WITHDRAWN

1st EDITION

Perspectives on Diseases and Disorders

Schizophrenia

Jacqueline Langwith
Book Editor

9/10

GALE
CENGAGE Learning

Detroit • New York • San Francisco • New Haven, Conn • Waterville, Maine • London

Christine Nasso, *Publisher*
Elizabeth Des Chenes, *Managing Editor*

© 2011 Greenhaven Press, a part of Gale, Cengage Learning

For more information, contact:
Greenhaven Press
27500 Drake Rd.
Farmington Hills, MI 48331-3535
Or you can visit our Internet site at gale.cengage.com

For product information and technology assistance, contact us at

Gale Customer Support, 1-800-877-4253
For permission to use material from this text or product, submit all requests online at www.cengage.com/permissions

Further permissions questions can be e-mailed to permissionrequest@cengage.com

Articles in Greenhaven Press anthologies are often edited for length to meet page requirements. In addition, original titles of these works are changed to clearly present the main thesis and to explicitly indicate the author's opinion. Every effort is made to ensure that Greenhaven Press accurately reflects the original intent of the authors. Every effort has been made to trace the owners of copyrighted material.

Cover image copyright © Phototake, Inc./Phototake—All rights reserved.

LIBRARY OF CONGRESS CATALOGING-IN-PUBLICATION DATA

Schizophrenia / Jacqueline Langwith, book editor.
    p. cm. -- (Perspectives on diseases and disorders)
 Includes bibliographical references and index.
 ISBN 978-0-7377-5003-4 (hardcover)
 1. Schizophrenia--Popular works. I. Langwith, Jacqueline.
 RC514.S334153 2010
 616.89'8--dc22

                                              2010018888

Printed in the United States of America
1 2 3 4 5 6 7 14 13 12 11 10

CONTENTS

FOREWORD

"Medicine, to produce health, has to examine disease."
—Plutarch

Independent research on a health issue is often the first step to complement discussions with a physician. But locating accurate, well-organized, understandable medical information can be a challenge. A simple Internet search on terms such as "cancer" or "diabetes," for example, returns an intimidating number of results. Sifting through the results can be daunting, particularly when some of the information is inconsistent or even contradictory. The Greenhaven Press series Perspectives on Diseases and Disorders offers a solution to the often overwhelming nature of researching diseases and disorders.

From the clinical to the personal, titles in the Perspectives on Diseases and Disorders series provide students and other researchers with authoritative, accessible information in unique anthologies that include basic information about the disease or disorder, controversial aspects of diagnosis and treatment, and first-person accounts of those impacted by the disease. The result is a well-rounded combination of primary and secondary sources that, together, provide the reader with a better understanding of the disease or disorder.

Each volume in Perspectives on Diseases and Disorders explores a particular disease or disorder in detail. Material for each volume is carefully selected from a wide range of sources, including encyclopedias, journals, newspapers, nonfiction books, speeches, government documents, pamphlets, organization newsletters, and position papers. Articles in the first chapter provide an authoritative, up-to-date overview that covers symptoms, causes and effects, treatments, cures, and medical advances. The second chapter presents a substantial number of opposing viewpoints on controversial treatments and other current debates relating to the volume topic. The third chapter offers a variety of personal perspectives on the disease or disorder. Patients, doctors, caregivers, and loved ones represent just some of the voices found in this narrative chapter.

Each Perspectives on Diseases and Disorders volume also includes:

- An **annotated table of contents** that provides a brief summary of each article in the volume.
- An **introduction** specific to the volume topic.
- Full-color **charts and graphs** to illustrate key points, concepts, and theories.
- Full-color **photos** that show aspects of the disease or disorder and enhance textual material.
- **"Fast Facts"** that highlight pertinent additional statistics and surprising points.
- A **glossary** providing users with definitions of important terms.
- A **chronology** of important dates relating to the disease or disorder.
- An annotated list of **organizations to contact** for students and other readers seeking additional information.
- A **bibliography** of additional books and periodicals for further research.
- A detailed **subject index** that allows readers to quickly find the information they need.

Whether a student researching a disorder, a patient recently diagnosed with a disease, or an individual who simply wants to learn more about a particular disease or disorder, a reader who turns to Perspectives on Diseases and Disorders will find a wealth of information in each volume that offers not only basic information, but also vigorous debate from multiple perspectives.

INTRODUCTION

Schizophrenia is a global disease. It has been found in every culture in the world, both primitive and industrial, since it was first described by Emil Kraepelin in 1887. Beginning in the late 1960s and extending into the twenty-first century, the World Health Organization (WHO) undertook a series of landmark studies in hope of revealing the similarities and differences of schizophrenia in different cultures. In every culture studied, the researchers found that for most people the prognosis for schizophrenia is actually good—they recover and go on to lead productive lives. This result challenged the long-held view that a diagnosis of schizophrenia is dire and hopeless. The studies also revealed several differences between cultures. One of the most notable differences was that the prognosis for individuals with schizophrenia was better in developing countries than in developed countries. This result was at first surprising to researchers; they expected the opposite to be true, since developed countries generally have more resources to treat schizophrenia. However, scientists soon embraced the premise and attributed the better outcomes in developing countries to stronger social inclusion. That people with schizophrenia in developing countries have better outcomes than those in developed countries generally has been accepted as a fact by the scientific community. However, the premise has recently been challenged by some researchers who believe it should be reexamined.

The WHO schizophrenia studies are considered landmarks in the field of psychiatry because of their size, timeline, and scope. Individuals with a diagnosis of

A Chinese woman suffering from schizophrenia sits alone in a Beijing mental health facility. China has only 575 mental health hospitals and only 130,000 nurses and doctors specializing in psychiatry. (Andrew Wong/Reuters/Landov)

schizophrenia were studied across continents and cultures. Research participants came from urban and rural settings in countries including China, Czechoslovakia, Colombia, Denmark, Germany, India, Japan, Nigeria, Russia, the United Kingdom (UK), and the United States. Scientists and mental health workers from different backgrounds and cultures collaborated in the studies. They used standardized procedures to compare the nature of schizophrenia—its prevalence, its symptoms, the characteristics of those afflicted with it, and its prognosis—across all the different cultures studied. Individuals with schizophrenia were followed for between twelve and twenty-six years to find out how well they were doing after their initial diagnosis. The WHO scientists hoped that by undertaking such immense studies of schizophrenia they could gain a better understanding of the disease and develop better methods to deal with it.

The results from the WHO studies consistently showed that positive outcomes for schizophrenia were more common in developing countries like India, Colombia, and Nigeria than they were in the United States, the UK, Russia, and other developed countries. The WHO studies categorized people into five groups based on how well they had "recovered" after their initial diagnosis of schizophrenia. The very first of the WHO studies, the International Pilot Study of Schizophrenia, found that 52 percent of schizophrenics in developing countries were in the "best" category of recovery compared with 39 percent in developed countries. A subsequent WHO study from the 1980s, called the *Determinants of Outcome of Severe Mental Disorder (DOSMD)*, had strikingly similar results—56 percent of those in the developing world were in the best outcome group compared with 39 percent of the participants from the developed countries.

Researchers tried to understand what the results of the WHO studies meant. They attributed the better outcomes for people in the developing world to more family involvement in treatment, fewer social role expectations, less stigma, and greater social acceptance. Observations made during the studies tended to support this conclusion. For instance, it was observed that schizophrenics in the developing world tended to be married while those in the developed world did not. The researchers noted that nearly three-quarters of schizophrenics studied in India were married at follow-up, compared with only one-third of individuals in developed countries. In a 2007 book compiling the results of all WHO schizophrenia studies, researchers Kim Hopper, Glynn Harrison, Aleksandar Janca, and Norman Sartorius provided an example of how someone with schizophrenia in a developing country is generally treated. They described what happened to a female patient with schizophrenia in India found wandering by someone from her village. According to the researchers, "A female patient who was participating in a center survey was found wandering aimlessly in a dilapidated condition in another village by someone from her own village. He felt that it was a slur on his village to see this woman roaming about and immediately took her back to his village, where everyone provided help in feeding, clothing, and caring for her." The researchers say that this story is typical of Indian culture and that it illustrates an important reason for better outcomes in developing countries.

Based on the WHO studies, scientists concluded that the prognosis for schizophrenia is largely affected by the strength of an individual's social relationships. Writing in the *Schizophrenia Bulletin* in 2008, Norman Sartorius, one of the primary WHO researchers, suggested that the strong social ties evident in developing world cultures may be lacking in highly industrialized countries and thus could be a major reason for the difference in prognosis. According to Sartorius, "The sobering experience of high rates of chronic disability and dependency associated with schizophrenia in high income countries, despite access to costly biomedical treatment, suggests that something essential to recovery is missing in the social fabric."

For many years, scientists accepted as fact the better outcomes for schizophrenia in developing countries that the WHO studies revealed. However, in 2008 a group of researchers from several different countries published an article questioning whether it was prudent to accept the WHO studies' premise as fact. In the article, published in the *Schizophrenia Bulletin*, Alex Cohen from Harvard University, Vikram Patel from the London School of Hygiene and Tropical Medicine, Rangaswamy Thara from the Schizophrenia Research Foundation in India, and Oye Gurefe from the University of Ibadan in Nigeria reviewed twenty-three independent, non-WHO studies about schizophrenia from around the world. They found that enough variation existed in the research results to justify a reexamination of the WHO results.

Among the results questioned by Cohen and the other researchers was the conclusion from the WHO studies that people with fewer mental health treatment resources do better than people with greater access to care. According to the researchers, "The WHO studies have led to the ironic observation that abundance cripples and that scarcity and collaborative social world[s] are responsible for better outcomes." By contrast, in the twenty-three studies they looked at, the researchers found that a lack of care was associated with poorer outcomes. They also found it odd that people in developing countries are more accepting of people with schizophrenia. They point to surveys and research in Nigeria, Ethiopia, and Africa suggesting that high levels of stigma are associated with mental illness. This seems to fly in the face of the WHO studies, which indicated that less stigma was found in developing countries. Based on these inconsistencies, Cohen and his associates urged scientists to do more research and reexamine the prognosis of schizophrenia in different cultures. According to the authors, "During the past 30 years, international psychiatry has embraced the notion that the course and outcome of schizophrenia is better in so-called 'developing' countries. We believe our review of 23 studies in 11 low- and middle-income countries, provides enough evidence to justify a reexamination of this axiom."

The question of whether people in developing countries have better recoveries from schizophrenia than individuals in developed countries is just one of many ongoing debates about the disease. In *Perspectives on Diseases and Disorders: Schizophrenia*, other debates about schizophrenia are presented, along with personal accounts from people affected by the disease and articles describing the latest medical and scientific knowledge about schizophrenia.

CHAPTER 1

Understanding Schizophrenia

An Overview of Schizophrenia

**Paula Ford-Martin, Teresa G. Odle, and
Angela M. Costello**

In the following article Paula Ford-Martin, Teresa G. Odle, and
Angela M. Costello provide an overview of the psychotic disorder
known as schizophrenia. According to the authors, schizophrenia
is a chronic and disabling mental disease marked by disturbances
in thinking, emotional responsiveness, and behavior. There is no
single cause of schizophrenia, and diagnosis is dependent on a
variety of symptoms, such as delusions, hallucinations, flattened
affect, or an inability to experience pleasure. Treatment typically
involves drug therapy and inpatient or outpatient programs. The
authors say that prognosis for schizophrenia is generally less positive than for other mental disorders. Ford-Martin, Odle, and Costello
are nationally published medical writers.

*Photo on facing page.
Schizophrenia has
no specific cause,
and diagnosis is
dependent on a variety
of symptoms, which
may include delusions,
hallucinations, and an
inability to experience
pleasure.* (George Mattei/
Photo Researchers, Inc.)

SOURCE: Paula Ford-Martin, Teresa G. Odle, and Angela M.
Costello, "Schizophrenia," *Gale Encyclopedia of Alternative Medicine*,
2009. Copyright © 2009 by Gale, Cengage Learning. Reproduced by
permission of Gale, a part of Cengage Learning.

The term *schizophrenia* comes from two Greek words that mean "split mind." It was coined around 1908, by the Swiss doctor Eugen Bleuler, to describe the splitting apart of mental functions that he regarded as the central characteristic of schizophrenia. (Note that the splitting apart of mental functions in schizophrenia differs from the split personality of people with multiple personality disorder.)

Schizophrenic patients are typically unable to filter sensory stimuli and may have enhanced perceptions of sounds, colors, and other features of their environment. If untreated, most people diagnosed with schizophrenia gradually withdraw from interactions with other people, and lose their ability to take care of personal needs and grooming.

Although schizophrenia was described by doctors as far back as Hippocrates (500 BC), it is difficult to classify. Some psychiatrists prefer to identify schizophrenia as a group or family of disorders, rather than a single entity, because of the lack of agreement in classification, as well as the possibility that different subtypes of the disorder may eventually be shown to have different causes.

Stages of Schizophrenia

The course of schizophrenia in adults can be divided into three phases or stages. In the acute phase, the patient has an overt loss of contact with reality (psychotic episode) that requires intervention and treatment. In the second or stabilization phase, the initial psychotic symptoms have been brought under control, but the patient is at risk for relapse if treatment is interrupted. In the third or maintenance phase, the patient is relatively stable and can be kept indefinitely on antipsychotic medications. Even in the maintenance phase, however, relapses are not unusual, and patients do not always return to full functioning.

The patient's first psychotic episode, in most cases, is preceded by a prodromal (warning) phase, with a vari-

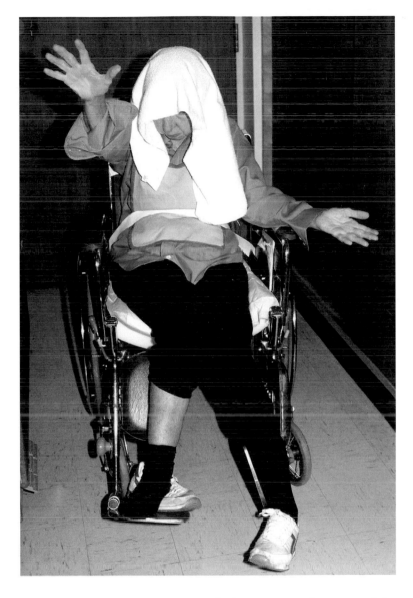

Schizophrenia is a chronic and disabling mental disease marked by disturbances in thinking and emotional responses and by acute behavior problems. (Grunnitus Studio/Photo Researchers, Inc.)

ety of behaviors that may include angry outbursts, withdrawal from social activities, loss of attention to personal hygiene and grooming, anhedonia (loss of one's capacity for enjoyment), and other unusual behaviors. There is no typical pattern or course of the disorder following the first acute episode. About 70% of patients diagnosed with schizophrenia have a second psychotic breakdown within five to seven years after the first one. About 10% of patients recover from the first psychotic episode and never experience another episode. About 55% of patients have chronic symptoms, and the remaining individuals have intermittent episodes over the course of their lives but can lead fairly normal lives otherwise.

Subtypes of Schizophrenia

A standard professional reference, the fourth revised (2000) edition of *The Diagnostic and Statistical Manual of Mental Disorders* [Revised Edition, Text Revision] *(DSM-IV-TR)* categorizes the five subtypes of schizophrenia as follows.

Paranoid.
The key feature of this subtype of schizophrenia is the combination of false beliefs (delusions) and hearing voices (auditory hallucinations), with relatively unaffected mood and cognitive functions (reasoning, judgment, and memory). The delusions of paranoid schizophrenics usually involve thoughts of being persecuted or harmed by others, or exaggerated opinions of their own importance, but may also reflect feelings of jealousy or excessive religiosity. The delusions are typically organized into a coherent framework. Paranoid schizophrenics function at a higher level than other subtypes but are at risk for suicidal or violent behavior under the influence of their delusions.

Disorganized.
Disorganized schizophrenia (formerly called hebephrenic schizophrenia) is marked by disorganized speech, thinking, and behavior, coupled with flat or inappropriate emotional responses to a situation (affect). The patient may act silly or withdraw socially to an extreme extent. Most patients in this category have weak personality structures prior to their initial acute psychotic delusions.

Catatonic.
Catatonic schizophrenia is characterized by disturbances of movement that may include rigidity, stupor, agitation,

bizarre posturing, and repetitive imitations of the movements or speech of other people. These patients are at risk for malnutrition, exhaustion, or self-injury. This subtype appears to be more common in non-Western countries than in Europe or North America. Catatonia as a symptom is most commonly associated with mood disorders.

Undifferentiated.
Patients in this category have the characteristic positive and negative symptoms of schizophrenia but do not meet the full criteria for the paranoid, disorganized, or catatonic subtypes.

Residual.
Patients in this category have had at least one acute schizophrenic episode, continue to have some negative symptoms of schizophrenia, but do not have current psychotic symptoms, such as delusions and hallucinations. They may have negative symptoms, such as withdrawal from others, or mild forms of positive symptoms, which indicate that the disorder has not completely resolved.

In the United States, Canada, and Western Europe, the sex ratio in schizophrenia is 1.4:1, with males being affected slightly more often than females. However, there is a significant gender difference in average age at onset; the average for males is between ages 18 and 25, whereas for women there are two peaks, one between ages 25 and 35 and a second rise in incidence after age 45. About 15% of all women who develop schizophrenia are diagnosed after age 35. In some women, the first symptoms of the disorder appear postpartum (after giving birth). Many women with schizophrenia are initially misdiagnosed as having depression or bipolar disorder because women with schizophrenia are likely to have more difficulties with emotional regulation than men with the disorder. In general, however, females have higher levels of functioning prior to symptom onset than males. . . .

Patient Age at the Onset of Schizophrenia

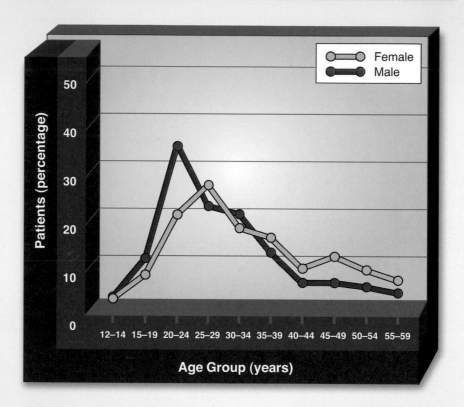

Taken from: Dwight B. Evans et al., eds., *Treating and Preventing Adolescent Mental Health Disorders.* New York: Oxford University Press, 2006.

No Single Cause of Schizophrenia

Schizophrenia is considered the end result of a combination of genetic, biochemical, developmental, and environmental factors, some of which are still not completely understood. There is no known single cause of the disorder.

Researchers have known for many years that first-degree biological relatives of patients with schizophrenia have a 10% risk of developing the disorder, as compared with 1% in the general population. The monozygotic (identical) twin of a person with schizophrenia has a 40 to 50% risk. The fact that this risk is not higher, however, indicates that environmental as well as genetic factors are implicated in the development of schizophrenia.

Some specific regions on certain human chromosomes have been linked to schizophrenia. However, these regions tend to vary across ethnic groups. Scientists are inclined to think that the genetic factors underlying schizophrenia vary across different ethnic groups, so that it is highly unlikely that susceptibility to the disorder is determined by only one gene. Because of this assumption, schizophrenia is considered a polygenic disorder.

Research conducted by the National Institute of Mental Health (NIMH) in 2007 suggested that certain genes create an imbalance between the pathways mediating D2 and D1 dopamine receptors, increasing the risk for schizophrenia.

Other studies conducted by the NIMH have demonstrated the existence of a connection between two abnormalities of brain functioning in patients with schizophrenia. The researchers used radioactive tracers and positron emission tomography (PET) to show that reduced activity in a part of the brain called the prefrontal cortex was associated in the patients, but not in the control subjects, with abnormally elevated levels of dopamine (a chemical that transmits signals in the brain) in the striatum. High levels of dopamine are related to the delusions and hallucinations of psychotic episodes in schizophrenia. These findings suggest that treatment directed at the prefrontal cortex might be more effective than present antipsychotic medications, which essentially target dopamine levels without regard to specific areas of the brain.

There is some evidence that schizophrenia may be a type of developmental disorder related to the formation of faulty connections between nerve cells during fetal development. The changes in the brain that normally occur during puberty then interact with these connections to trigger the symptoms of the disorder. Other researchers have suggested that a difficult childbirth may result in developmental vulnerabilities that eventually lead to schizophrenia.

Certain environmental factors during pregnancy are also associated with an increased risk of schizophrenia in the offspring. These include the mother's exposure to starvation or famine, influenza during the second trimester of pregnancy, and Rh incompatibility [a blood-type difference between mother and fetus] in a second or third pregnancy.

Some researchers are investigating a possible connection between schizophrenia and viral infections of the hippocampus, a structure in the brain that is associated with memory formation and the human stress response. It is thought that damage to the hippocampus might account for the sensory disturbances found in schizophrenia. Another line of research related to viral causes of schizophrenia concerns a protein deficiency in the brain.

Environmental stressors related to home and family life (e.g., parental death or divorce, family dysfunction) or to separation from the family of origin in late adolescence (e.g., going away to college or military training; marriage) may trigger the onset of schizophrenia in individuals with genetic or psychological vulnerabilities.

Symptoms of Schizophrenia

The onset of symptoms in schizophrenia may be either abrupt (sudden) or insidious (gradual). Often, however, it goes undetected for two to three years after the onset of symptoms because the symptoms occur in the context of a previous history of cognitive and behavioral problems. The patient may have had panic attacks, social phobia, or substance abuse problems, any of which can complicate the process of diagnosis. Patients with schizophrenia do not always have the same set of symptoms, and each patient's symptoms may change over time.

The symptoms of schizophrenia are divided into two major categories: positive and negative.

The positive symptoms of schizophrenia are defined by *DSM*-IV as excesses or distortions of normal mental functions. The positive symptoms of schizophrenia include four "first-rank" or Schneiderian symptoms, named for the German psychiatrist Kurt Schneider who proposed these symptoms as diagnostic of the disorder in 1959. Positive symptoms include:

- delusions
- somatic hallucinations
- hearing voices commenting on one's behavior or talking to each other
- thought insertion or withdrawal

Delusions are false but strongly held beliefs that result from the patient's inability to separate real from unreal events. The most common form of delusion in patients with schizophrenia is persecutory; individuals believe that others—family members, clinical staff, terrorists—are victimizing them. Another common delusion is referential, which means that the person interprets objects or occurrences in the environment (e.g., a picture on the wall, a song played on the radio, laughter in the corridor) as being directed at or referring to them.

Hallucinations are disturbances of sense perception. Somatic hallucinations refer to sensations or perceptions about one's body that have no known medical cause, such as the notion that one's brain is radioactive.

Auditory hallucinations (e.g., hearing voices) are the most common form of hallucination in schizophrenia, although visual, tactile, olfactory, and gustatory hallucinations may also occur.

Thought insertion and/or withdrawal refer to delusions that other beings or forces (e.g., God, the FBI, the CIA, Martians) have the power to put thoughts or ideas into one's mind or remove them. . . .

The negative symptoms of schizophrenia represent a loss or reduction of normal functioning, according to the *DSM*-IV. Negative symptoms represent the lack or absence of behaviors and include:

- *Blunted or flattened affect.* This term refers to loss of emotional expressiveness. The person's face may be unresponsive or expressionless, and speech may lack vitality or warmth.
- *Alogia.* Alogia is sometimes called poverty of speech. The person has little to say and is not able to expand on his or her statements. A doctor examining the patient must be able to distinguish between alogia and unwillingness to speak.
- *Avolition.* The person is unable to begin or stay with goal-directed activities. The person may sit in one location for long periods of time or show little interest in joining group activities.
- *Anhedonia.* Anhedonia refers to the loss of one's capacity for enjoyment or pleasure.

In general, the negative symptoms are more difficult for doctors to evaluate than the positive symptoms because they may be influenced by a concurrent depressive disorder or a dull and unstimulating environment. However, negative symptoms account for much of the morbidity (unhealthiness) associated with schizophrenia. . . .

Diagnosis Based on Many Symptoms

There are no symptoms that are unique to schizophrenia, and no single symptom that is a diagnostic hallmark of the disorder. In addition, there are no laboratory tests or imaging tests that can establish or confirm a diagnosis of schizophrenia. The diagnosis is based on a constellation or group of related symptoms that are, according to *DSM*-IV-TR, "associated with impaired occupational or social functioning."

As part of the process of diagnosis, the doctor takes a careful medical history and orders laboratory tests of the patient's blood or urine in order to rule out general medical conditions or substance abuse disorders that may be accompanied by disturbed behavior. X rays or other imaging studies of the head may also be ordered. Medical conditions to be ruled out include epilepsy, head trauma, brain tumor, Cushing's syndrome, Wilson's disease, Huntington's disease, and encephalitis. Drugs of abuse that may cause symptoms resembling schizophrenia include amphetamines (speed), cocaine, and phencyclidine (PCP). In older patients, dementia and delirium must be ruled out. If the patient has held jobs involving exposure to mercury, polychlorinated biphenyls (PCBs), or other toxic substances, environmental poisoning must also be considered in the differential diagnosis.

The doctor must also rule out other mental disorders that may be accompanied by psychotic symptoms, such as mood disorders; brief psychotic disorders; dissociative disorder not otherwise specified or dissociative identity disorder; delusional disorder; schizotypal, schizoid, or paranoid personality disorders; and pervasive developmental disorders. In children, childhood-onset schizophrenia must be distinguished from communication disorders with disorganized speech and from attention-deficit/hyperactivity disorder.

After other organic and mental disorders have been ruled out, it must be determined whether the patient meets the following criteria, as specified by *DSM-IV-TR*:

> **FAST FACT**
>
> According to the National Institute of Mental Health, schizophrenia affects 1.1% of the American population over age eighteen.

- *Presence of positive and negative symptoms.* The patient must have two (or more) of the following symptoms during a one-month period: delusions; hallucinations; disorganized speech; disorganized or catatonic behavior; negative symptoms.
- *Decline in social, interpersonal, or occupational functioning,* including personal hygiene or self-care.

- *Duration.* The symptomatic behavior must last for at least six months.
- *Diagnostic exclusions.* Mood disorders, substance abuse disorders, medical conditions, and developmental disorders have been ruled out.

Treatment Primarily Involves Medication

In the late 2000s treatment of schizophrenia focused on symptom reduction and relapse prevention, since the causes of the disorder had not yet been clearly identified. Unfortunately, not all patients with schizophrenia receive adequate treatment.

Antipsychotic medications are the primary treatment for schizophrenia. Drug therapy for the disorder, however, is complicated by several factors: the unpredictability of a given patient's response to specific medications, the number of potentially troublesome side effects, the high rate of substance abuse among patients with schizophrenia, and the possibility of drug interactions between antipsychotic medications and antidepressants or other medications that may be prescribed for the patient.

One of the most difficult challenges in treating schizophrenia patients with medications is helping them stay on medication. Many schizophrenics do not take their medication because it does not adequately control their symptoms or produces adverse side effects. After the patient has been stabilized, an antipsychotic drug may be given in a long-acting form called a depot dose. Depot medications last for two to four weeks; they have the advantage of protecting the patient against the consequences of forgetting or skipping daily doses. In addition, some patients who do not respond to oral neuroleptics have better results with depot form.

The first antipsychotic medications for schizophrenia were introduced in the 1950s and known as dopamine antagonists (DAs). Sometimes called neuroleptics, they include haloperidol (Haldol), chlorpromazine (Thorazine), perphenazine (Trilafon), and fluphenazine (Pro-lixin). About 40% of patients, however, fail to respond to treatment with these medications. Neuroleptics can control most of the positive symptoms of schizophrenia as well as reduce the frequency and severity of relapses, but they have little effect on negative symptoms. In addition, these medications have problematic side effects, ranging from dry mouth, blurry vision, and restlessness (akathisia) to such long-term side effects as tardive dyskinesia (TD), a disorder characterized by involuntary movements of the mouth, lips, arms, or legs. TD affects about 15 to 20% of patients who have been receiving neuroleptic medications over a period of years. Discomfort related to these side effects is one reason why 40% of patients treated with the older antipsychotics do not adhere to their medication regimens.

The atypical antipsychotics are newer medications introduced in the 1990s. They are sometimes called serotonin dopamine antagonists (SDAs). These medications include aripiprazole (Abilify), clozapine (Clozaril), risperidone (Risperdal), quetiapine (Seroquel), ziprasidone (Geodon), and olanzapine (Zyprexa). These drugs are more effective in treating the negative symptoms of schizophrenia and have fewer side effects than the previous antipsychotics. Clozapine has been reported to be effective in patients who do not respond to neuroleptics, and it helps to reduce the risk of suicide attempts. The atypical antipsychotics, however, do have weight gain as a side effect, and patients taking clozapine must have their blood monitored periodically for signs of agranulocytosis (a drop in the number of white blood cells). . . .

In- and Outpatient Treatment

Patients with schizophrenia are usually hospitalized during acute psychotic episodes, to prevent harming themselves or others, and to begin treatment with antipsychotic medications. A patient having a first psychotic episode is usually given a computed tomography (CT) or magnetic resonance imaging (MRI) scan to rule out structural brain disease.

Since the 1990s, patients with schizophrenia who have been stabilized on antipsychotic medications have been given psychosocial therapies of various types to assist them with motivation, self-care, and forming relationships with others. In addition, because many patients have had their education or vocational training interrupted by the onset of the disorder, they may be helped by therapies directed toward improving their social functioning and work skills.

Specific outpatient treatments that have been used with patients with schizophrenia include:

- *Rehabilitation programs.* These programs may offer vocational counseling, job training, problem-solving, and money management skills, use of public transportation, and social skills training.
- *Cognitive-behavioral therapy and supportive psychotherapy.*
- *Family psychoeducation.* This approach is intended to help family members understand the patient's illness, cope with the problems it creates for other family members, and minimize stresses that may increase the patient's risk of relapse.
- *Self-help groups.* These groups provide mutual support for family members as well as patients. They can also serve as advocacy groups for better research and treatment, and to protest social stigma and employment discrimination. . . .

The Prognosis for Schizophrenia

Patients with early onset of schizophrenia are more often male, have a lower level of functioning prior to onset, a higher rate of brain abnormalities, more noticeable negative symptoms, and worse outcomes. Patients with later onset are more likely to be female, with fewer brain abnormalities and thought impairment, and more hopeful prognoses.

The average course and outcome for people with schizophrenia are less favorable than those for most other mental disorders. About 20% of patients with schizophrenia recover the full level of functioning that they had before the onset of the disorder, according to NIMH statistics, but the remaining 80% have problems reentering mainstream society. These patients are often underachievers in school and in the workplace, and they usually have difficulty forming healthy relationships with others. The majority (60–70%) of patients with schizophrenia do not marry or have children, and most have very few friends or social contacts. The impact of these social difficulties as well as the stress caused by the symptoms themselves is reflected in the high suicide rate among patients with schizophrenia. About 10% commit suicide within the first 10 years after their diagnosis—a rate 20 times higher than that of the general population.

Schizophrenics with a high number of stressful changes in their lives, or who have frequent contacts with critical or emotionally involved family members, are more likely to relapse. Overall, the most important component of long-term care for schizophrenic patients is their compliance with their regimen of antipsychotic medications.

The Genetic Cause of Schizophrenia

Emily Singer

In the following selection Emily Singer describes what appears to be a genetic link to schizophrenia, mental retardation, and autism. According to Singer, scientists think small mistakes in a region of DNA called "1q21.1" may play a role in causing schizophrenia, mental retardation, and autism. This discovery could lead to new medications to treat these disorders and new tests to help doctors diagnose them. Singer is the biotechnology and life science editor at *Technology Review*.

G o about 145,000,000 bases (or "letters") down the long arm of chromosome 1 and you'll come to 1q21.1, the genetic address of a small but important piece of DNA that is particularly prone to mistakes. When chromosome 1 is duplicated during normal cell division (say, in creating sperm or eggs), short, repetitive

SOURCE: Emily Singer, "A Hole in the Genome," *Technology Review*, vol. 112, March/April 2009, pp. 82–83. Copyright © 2009 by the Association of Alumni and Alumnae of MIT. Reproduced by permission.

bits of DNA within this stretch are all too likely to mistakenly pair up, raising the chances that the new cells will have extra or missing copies of specific pieces of DNA.

Small Mistake, Big Impact

Those small mistakes can have a big impact on people who carry them. Several studies in the last year [2008 to early 2009] have found that missing or extra pieces of DNA in the 1q21.1 region put the bearer at risk for a surprisingly broad range of psychiatric and neurological disorders, including autism, schizophrenia, and mental retardation. The discovery that one piece of DNA can lead to such diverse outcomes is opening new avenues in the study of disease. Rather than focusing solely on finding a common genetic flaw in everyone with a particular disease, researchers have begun to examine the various consequences that the same genetic flaw may have in different people. These studies suggest that even patients with different diagnoses may share common biological problems. "It's been eye-opening," says Mark Daly, a geneticist at the Broad Institute in Cambridge, Massachusetts, "because it's made us realize that in searching for the molecular basis of disease, it may be profitable to search for connections between seemingly unrelated phenotypes [observable physical or biochemical characteristics]." Last year [2008], Daly and his colleagues identified a section of DNA on chromosome 16 that also raises the risk of several different brain disorders, suggesting that this pattern may be common in the genetics of disease.

Physicians have long known that structural abnormalities in our genomes—deletions duplications, and rearrangements of large stretches of DNA—trigger developmental problems and disease. Down syndrome, for example, results from an extra copy of chromosome 21. But over the last few years, new kinds of microarrays—small slides dotted with specific sequences of DNA—have begun allowing scientists to efficiently search the genome for architectural flaws too small to be visible with a microscope. These errors, called copy number variations, are distinct from the single-letter changes that until recently have been the focus of most research into genetic variation. Ranging in size from one thousand to more than one million base pairs, they can encompass part of a gene or one or more entire genes.

Genomic Hot Spot

The far end of region 1q21.1, which at about one million bases long constitutes a tiny percentage of the roughly 3.2 billion pairs of letters that make up human DNA, harbors just one of the genome's many "hot spots"—so called for their tendency toward structural instability. But in this region, structural abnormalities—especially missing sequences—seem particularly troublesome. Intrigued by this mysterious morsel of DNA, Heather Mefford, a pediatric geneticist at the University of Washington in Seattle, compiled data on variations in 1q21.1 from clinical genetics labs around the world. She found that 25 patients in a sample of more than 5,000 people with autism, mental retardation, or other congenital abnormalities were missing the same chunk within the region. While that is a small percentage, no one in a similar-sized group of healthy people carried that particular mistake, meaning that the deletion is the likely cause—or at least partial cause—of the patients' problems. Studies by other researchers have linked similar changes in the region to schizophrenia, as well as to abnormal head size and accompanying developmental delays.

Different studies linking 1q21.1 to mental retardation, autism, and schizophrenia all identified deletions or duplications in approximately the same region. That's because this particular stretch is flanked by repetitive sequences prone to rearrangement. It contains at least eight known genes, the functions of which are mostly

unknown. "This region of the genome must clearly have one or more genes that are important for normal cognitive development," says Mefford, whose research was published in the *New England Journal of Medicine* in October [2008].

Scientists hope that identifying the underlying mechanisms affected by the missing or duplicated piece of DNA will provide new targets for drug development. But at this point, it's not clear whether it's one gene or several that raise the risk of disease, or how deletions and duplications of the same piece of DNA can trigger outcomes as different as schizophrenia and mental retardation.

Common Biological Underpinnings

The findings do hint that autism, schizophrenia, and mental retardation have common biologic underpinnings, a conclusion that has some precedent. Children with mental retardation often have psychiatric and behavioral problems as well, although these may be undiagnosed or underappreciated in the face of their cognitive deficits. And some families may have a history of mental illness, but not of a specific illness.

Mental retardation, autism, and (to some extent) schizophrenia are developmental diseases, diagnosed in childhood or adolescence. So identifying a common biological flaw may shed light on the crucial components of neural development and suggest ways to help when that development goes awry. Perhaps a disruption in the 1q21.1 region of the chromosome inherited from one parent can send some fundamental developmental process off course. The ultimate impact might depend on environmental factors, variations in other parts of the genome, or the version of the gene inherited from the other parent. Someone whose genome has mistakes in other

> **FAST FACT**
>
> Studies of identical twins show that when one twin has schizophrenia, the other twin will have it nearly 50 percent of the time.

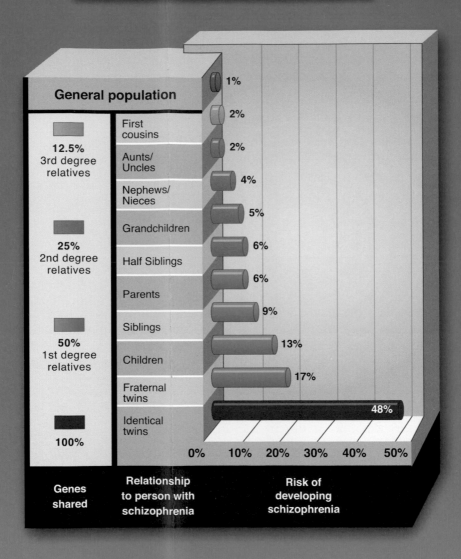

Heredity of Schizophrenia

General population

Genes shared

12.5% 3rd degree relatives	
25% 2nd degree relatives	
50% 1st degree relatives	
100%	

Relationship to person with schizophrenia

Relationship	Risk of developing schizophrenia
	1%
First cousins	2%
Aunts/ Uncles	2%
Nephews/ Nieces	4%
Grandchildren	5%
Half Siblings	6%
Parents	6%
Siblings	9%
Children	13%
Fraternal twins	17%
Identical twins	48%

0%   10%   20%   30%   40%   50%

Risk of developing schizophrenia

Taken from: Schizophrenia.com, "Heredity and the Genetics of Schizophrenia." www.schizophrenia.com.

regions that are important for brain development and cognitive function might end up with mental retardation. Someone whose genome is largely intact, but who has a mutation in a gene linked to autism, may end up with high-functioning autism.

Research May Lead to a Diagnostic Test

A better understanding of the molecular consequences of errors in 1q21.1 and other recently identified hot spots may help redefine autism and schizophrenia and even change the way they are diagnosed. Both disorders cause a wide range of symptoms, and they are currently identified through behavioral and cognitive tests. Physicians may now be able to augment that diagnosis with the results of genetic testing. Only a small percentage of people with autism or schizophrenia will carry a particular genetic variation. But researchers hope that as more copy number variations are linked to these disorders, such genetic characterizations will become useful tools for predicting the best treatment for a given patient.

"At one time in the history of medicine, when you had a cough and an infection of the lungs, they called it pneumonia," says James Lupski, a physician and scientist at Baylor College of Medicine. Now we know that

Physicians may now be able to augment the diagnosis of schizophrenia through genetic testing and analysis of patients' DNA. (© Deco Images II/ Alamy)

pneumonia is actually a group of different diseases, both bacterial and viral, that must each be treated differently. Eventually, someone developed a way to distinguish bacterial pneumonia from other forms, Lupski says, and that set the stage for the development of different treatments.

A diagnostic test that can detect copy number variations already exists: array CGH, the same test scientists use in research studies. It is currently used in clinical genetics labs to diagnose unexplained cases of mental retardation, developmental delay, and, increasingly, autism as well. It's not yet clear how to use the results to guide treatment—especially in disorders such as autism, for which no drugs are available to treat the root cause. But when it comes to other disorders, scientists are optimistic. "We have lots of effective psychiatric drugs, but it often takes weeks to find the right one," says Lupski. "Could this simple characterization predict the one that works best? That alone would be of tremendous benefit to patients."

The Risks of Schizophrenia Associated with Fetal Development

Emily Laber-Warren

In the following selection Emily Laber-Warren asserts that the risks of a person's developing schizophrenia may be influenced by environmental stressors that occur very early in development. Laber-Warren says pregnant women who experience an extremely stressful event are more likely to have children who will become schizophrenic. Additionally, says Laber-Warren, pregnant women who get the flu could also be at an increased risk of having a child who becomes schizophrenic. According to Laber-Warren, scientists are finding that maternal nutrition, stress, and other influences can impact fetal development and contribute to the cause of disorders such as schizophrenia and autism. Laber-Warren is a writer and editor who contributes to *Scientific American Mind*, *Psychology Today*, and other publications.

I prided myself on being low-key about my pregnancy. I didn't read *What to Expect When You're Expecting*—OK, so I bought a copy, but I only used it as a reference. I traveled, I socialized, and I worked full-time until

SOURCE: Emily Laber-Warren, "A Fateful First Act," *Psychology Today,* May/June 2009, pp. 84–87. Copyright © 2009 Sussex Publishers LLC. Reproduced by permission.

five days before giving birth, even though I was carrying twins. I did not want to believe that anything essential about me had changed. That is, until the night I shook my husband from sleep, sobbing hysterically, convinced that by eating a few pieces of feta cheese I had irreversibly damaged our babies.

I had read that some cheeses could harbor a bacterium called Listeria that causes birth defects. But I rebelled. All these prohibitions directed at my most innocent pleasures! I'd already cut out wine, coffee, sushi, bike riding, and countless other things I enjoyed. When I was six months pregnant, I got sick after gorging on a cheese plate at an office party. In the midst of my ensuing panic—would my children suffer their whole lives for one dumb, piggy move of mine?—something clicked: These fetuses weren't veteran humans. They were different, and painfully vulnerable.

Everyone knows by now that it's bad for women to smoke or drink while pregnant, but a large body of research is revealing that much more subtle influences, such as being anemic, feeling perpetually stressed, or simply getting the flu, can also harm a developing baby. "It's a new understanding of what causes vulnerability to disease," says Vivette Glover, a perinatal psychobiologist at Imperial College London.

Until recently, doctors believed that the journey from fertilized egg to baby followed unwavering genetic instructions. But a flood of new studies reveals that fetal development is a complicated duet between the baby's genes and the messages it receives from its mother. Based on those signals, the fetus chooses one path over another, often resulting in long-term changes—to the structure of its kidneys, say, or how sensitive its brain will be to the chemical dopamine, which plays a role in mood, motivation, and reward.

This new science of fetal programming, which investigates how in utero influences cause physiological

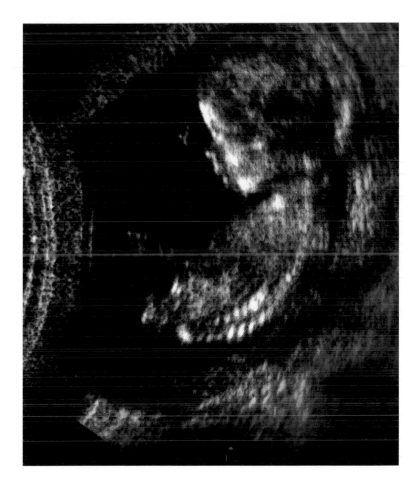

Ultrasound fetal scans are used in the new science of fetal programming, which studies how in utero influences can cause physiological changes that linger later in life. **(Zephyr/Photo Researchers, Inc.)**

changes that can linger into later life, is producing clues to mysterious disorders such as autism and schizophrenia, as well as evidence of the very early effects of stress and toxins. Scientists still don't know all the hows and whys of these fetal cues, but the when is very clear: earlier than we ever thought.

A Delicate Project

Our first nine months resonate for the next 70 or 80 years because the fetal enterprise is so enormously ambitious. In just 270 days, a single cell becomes trillions of diverse and specialized cells—that's more cells than there are galaxies in the universe. As in any construction project, events unfold in a highly coordinated sequence. Each cell not only has its own job to do, it spurs other cells to action—sending out chemical signals that tell its neighbors to divide like crazy or to self-destruct. So when something goes wrong it can set off a domino effect. Cells might not travel to their intended destination, or they might stop multiplying too soon, or, in the case of brain cells, they might fail to establish the right interconnections.

"We pass more biological milestones before we're born than at any other time in our lives," says Peter Nathanielsz, director of the Center for Pregnancy and Newborn Research at the University of Texas Health Science Center at San Antonio. "If we do not pass them correctly, there is a price to pay."

Pregnancy is a dynamic process; the fetus is attuned to its mother in many ways. It learns about the day-night cycle from her rhythm of sleep and activity. It knows her voice: A classic 1980 study showed that immediately after birth, infants prefer a recording of their own mother reading a book over that of another woman reading the same story. The fetus even comes to appreciate its mother's taste in food after swallowing gallons of amniotic fluid tinged with those flavors. "The fetus is already a learning organism," says Christopher Coe, a psychologist at the University of Wisconsin–Madison.

By the same token, if its mother fails to provide vital nutrients, the fetus prepares for a world of scarcity, adjusting its metabolism so that it can wring the most out of every calorie. Such a baby might be born with a liver and pancreas that have less capacity to process fats and sugars, predisposing the adult to high cholesterol levels and diabetes. If the mom's stress hormones are high, her baby prepares to enter a harsh world—recalibrating its brain and nervous system to be on high alert for potential threats. As the years pass, the

FAST FACT

According to studies, about seven in every one thousand people will develop schizophrenia.

alterations that took place in the womb—especially when coupled with an unlucky genetic inheritance, a troubled upbringing, or an unhealthy lifestyle—may lead to problems: Heart attack. Diabetes. Osteoporosis. Depression. Schizophrenia.

Frazzled Origins

The womb experience helps establish a child's emotional resilience and susceptibility to disease, and unfortunately, that experience is not always completely under the mother's control.

If a woman is anxious for months at a time—say she's in a troubled marriage or is financially strapped—high levels of the stress hormone cortisol may reach her fetus. Such a fetus doesn't need as many brain receptors to sense the hormone's presence, so it develops fewer. But having fewer cortisol receptors changes a person's ability to cope in later life. The cortisol system has its own shut-off valve; when cortisol levels in the bloodstream reach a certain point, the body stops making the hormone and everything returns to normal. But people with fewer receptors don't sense that it's time to stop making cortisol until they're practically swimming in it. Living with high levels of cortisol not only creates wear and tear on the body but also makes it tough to handle strong emotions without lashing out or withdrawing, and it may set people up for depression.

Infants whose pregnant mothers developed post-traumatic stress disorder after the September 11 [2001 terrorist] attacks were found to be more easily upset by loud noises and unfamiliar people. "Temperament is not only genetically determined," says Catherine Monk, a Columbia University psychologist. "It is constructed throughout early development and, in part, in utero by exposure to the mother's mood." In a study of thousands of women in England, those who ranked in the top 15 percent for anxiety during pregnancy had children with

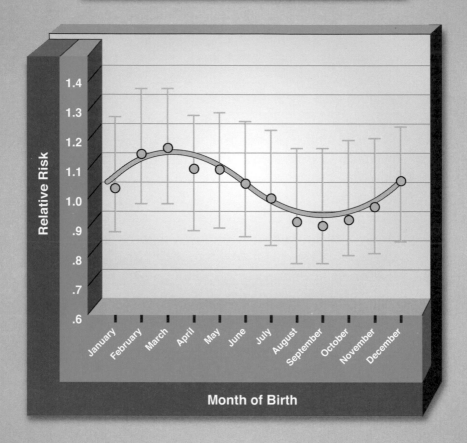

Relative Risk of Schizophrenia According to Month of Birth

Month of Birth

Taken from: Schizophrenia.com, "Season of Birth—Low Sunlight Exposure/Vitamin D Deficiency Is Associated with Higher Risk of Schizophrenia." www.schizophrenia.com.

double the rate of emotional and behavioral problems at 10 years old.

Stress may cause long-term cognitive deficiencies, too. Coe subjects pregnant monkeys to three loud carhorn bursts at unpredictable intervals over a 10-minute period, and he does it daily for one-quarter of their pregnancy. "Certainly women living in the Congo or in Iraq have a much more stressful pregnancy than anything I ever studied," he says. Yet even this moderate amount of stress results in infant monkeys that are less able to hold up their heads or scrutinize novel objects. At three years old, their hippocampus, a brain area responsible for learning and memory, is 10 percent smaller than normal, which likely translates into worse functioning.

Just as challenges can bring out the best in adults, prenatal stress seems to benefit children sometimes: Two-year-olds whose mothers were moderately anxious or depressed during pregnancy performed better than average on reasoning and coordination tasks such as solving puzzles, stacking blocks, and manipulating small objects. It may be that moderately emotionally "charged" women provided a more varied intrauterine environment, with stimulations that sped up brain development.

On the other hand, one of the scariest risks for stressed-out pregnant women is the greater chance that their child will one day be schizophrenic. Israeli girls who were in their second month in the womb during the 1967 Arab-Israeli war were 4.3 times more likely to become schizophrenic than girls born at other times, and boys were 1.2 times more likely to develop the disease. Another study found that children of women who experienced the death of a close relative during the first trimester of pregnancy were also more likely to later develop schizophrenia.

Researchers speculate that the placenta is very sensitive to stress hormones coursing through a severely stressed-out mother's body, and that those hormones cause alterations in the fetal brain that help unleash schizophrenia down the line.

The First Forty Days

If a woman gets the flu during her first trimester, her child is seven times as likely to develop schizophrenia as a teenager or young adult. It may not be the flu itself that causes the malfunction, but rather an immunological reaction. Cytokines—proteins the mother's body produces in response to the flu—get transmitted to the fetus and harm its brain.

What is really intriguing is that mice that were given a specific cytokine, interleukin-6, gave birth to offspring who not only displayed schizophrenic-like behaviors but also behaviors analogous to those seen in autistic humans.

A 2008 study suggests that 12 to 15 percent of autism cases may occur because maternal autoantibodies—antibodies that a person makes against something in themselves—interfere with proteins in the fetal brain. After identifying unusual antibodies in women who had more than one autistic child, researchers injected the antibodies into four pregnant monkeys. They also gave antibodies taken from women with healthy children to another four pregnant monkeys. The offspring of the monkey mothers who received the regular antibodies were fine, but all four of those whose mothers got the unusual autoantibodies spontaneously developed bizarre tics, such as pacing and doing repeated backflips. "Repetition of motor behaviors is one of the three cardinal features of autism," says David Amaral, a neuroscientist at the M.I.N.D. Institute at the University of California, Davis, who headed the study. Scientists don't know under which conditions these autoantibodies form, nor why they do so.

They do know that a critical window for development is 20 to 40 days after fertilization. During that time, fetuses that eventually develop autism or schizophrenia often begin to display shared physical characteristics, such as protruding ears and unusual toes.

A groundbreaking idea could hold the answer to the puzzle of why some children are autistic while others become schizophrenic. Researchers Bernard Crespi and Christopher Badcock argue that a struggle between genes from Dad's sperm and Mom's eggs results in different expressions of the same genes. When a genetic region that plays a role in brain development is disrupted, the theory says, if the genes inherited from the father dominate, the disruption gives rise to autism, whereas if the genes inherited from the mother dominate, the interference will result in schizophrenia.

Quality of (In Utero) Life Issues

A fetus's only source of sustenance is the food and oxygen its mother takes in, and its access to those supplies can be precarious. The mom's meals nourish her first, then travel a winding path—through temporarily expanded uterine arteries to the greedy placenta, and finally along the rope-like umbilical cord.

If a mother eats a low-calorie or low-protein diet, or one deficient in essential fats or critical nutrients, such as folic acid, vitamin D, or iron, a fetus may lack the raw materials it needs to properly build its brain and other organs. (Iron-deficient infants are shyer, fussier, and less sociable.) Children born to women who are pregnant during a famine, for example, are more susceptible to heart disease and depression when they grow up. Starved fetuses build smaller organs with fewer blood vessels, which can lead to high blood pressure later on. Animal research suggests that not eating enough in the first days after conception can increase the potential for cardiovascular disease and diabetes, which is why women should eat well while trying to get pregnant.

But eating too much is also risky. When women gain more than the recommended weight during pregnancy (25 to 35 pounds for healthy women), their kids are 48 percent more likely to be overweight at the age of seven. A high-fat diet during pregnancy reshapes rat offspring's brains, making them crave fatty foods and putting them at risk for life-long obesity.

The negative effects of drinking while pregnant are well-known: Alcohol can damage key areas of the fetal brain, including the prefrontal cortex—the region responsible for planning, decision-making, and emotional restraint. What's new and disturbing is research showing that imbibing just a couple of drinks a day during the first 50 days after conception, when a woman may not yet know she is pregnant, creates the strongest effects.

Chemicals that lurk invisibly in our clothes and furniture, in the food we eat, and in the air we breathe dominate today's world. Some, like bisphenol A, a compound in some plastic water and baby bottles, resemble hormones such as estrogen that are produced by our own bodies, which makes them potentially harmful even at very low levels because the body is primed to respond to them. There is concern that the increase in abnormalities of newborn boys' reproductive organs—the rate of hypospadias, a birth defect of the urethra, doubled in the U.S. between 1970 and 1993—results from maternal exposure to such chemicals.

Faith, Love, and Compensation

My sons were born free of Listeria, and in fact were healthy in every way. But I now realize that there could be hidden problems. Twins have a harder time in utero because a mother can supply only so much food and oxygen, and they must share it. On top of that, this was my first pregnancy and I was over 35—factors that limit the stretchiness of the blood vessels that shuttle oxygen and nutrients to the uterus. Let's just say my fetuses were getting their supplies through a coffee stirrer instead of a straw.

And yet I remind myself: Birth is a beginning, not an ending. Nurturing and mental stimulation can reverse the effects of a compromised pregnancy. Monk and colleagues found that 4-month-old infants had high levels of stress hormones in their saliva when their mothers were anxious or depressed before the birth *and* unresponsive afterward. But when moms were attuned to their babies, the infants' cortisol levels were normal, no matter what the pregnancy was like.

If children learn good exercise and eating habits, they are unlikely to become obese or get diabetes. If their parents and other caregivers engage and nurture them, it is less likely they will develop learning or conduct disorders. "You can look at it as though the system has been primed," says Marta Weinstock-Rosin, a psychopharmacologist at Hebrew University in Jerusalem. "But if nothing else bad happens and everything is calm, it may well be all right."

And with an enriched upbringing, a compromised prenatal environment might even be turned to advantage. When brain development has been altered because a pregnant woman was highly anxious, drank martinis, or ate too much mercury-tainted fish, the resulting baby may be high-strung and hard to soothe. But the same sensitivity that leads to moodiness can also confer empathy and awareness. "You might just be more able to take in what's around you and actually do even better than average," Monk says.

Still, there's no getting around the fact that a mother's experiences profoundly shape her developing baby. Now that I know this, would I live my pregnancy differently? Absolutely. I would have eaten organic as much as possible to reduce my fetuses' exposure to toxins. To ensure that they had all the essential building blocks to grow healthy brain tissue, I would have poured flaxseed oil over my cereal and served up kale and broccoli almost every night. I would have begun taking prenatal vitamins and iron before getting pregnant. And imagining those little guys depending on me for all their oxygen, I would have thrown myself into yoga and spent 10 minutes every morning and evening taking deep breaths.

But I also remind myself of what I did right—a fair amount, judging from the mischievous, affectionate 2-year-olds my boys have become. "To have a baby is a huge affirmation and commitment to life and love," Monk says. Besides doing their best to stay healthy, mothers have no choice but to take a big leap of faith.

A Brain Protein Is Implicated as a Possible Cause of Schizophrenia

Marla Paul

In the following selection Marla Paul discusses the research findings of schizophrenia researchers at Northwestern University in Illinois. According to Paul, researchers at the university have discovered that schizophrenic mice had low levels of a brain protein called kalirin, which is important for building the vast network of nerve cells in the brain. Paul says that the discovery of kalirin may lead to new treatments for schizophrenia. Paul is the health sciences editor for the *Northwestern University NewsCenter.*

Schizophrenia waits silently until a seemingly normal child becomes a teenager or young adult. Then it swoops down and derails a young life.

Scientists have not understood what causes the severe mental disorder, which affects up to 1 percent of the population and results in hallucinations, memory loss and social withdrawal.

But new research from the Northwestern University Feinberg School of Medicine has revealed how schizophrenia works in the brain and provided a fresh opportunity for treatment. In a new, genetically engineered mouse model, scientists have discovered the disease symptoms are triggered by a low level of a brain protein necessary for neurons to talk to one another.

A Traffic Jam in the Brain

In human and mouse brains, kalirin is the brain protein needed to build the dense network of highways, called dendritic spines, which allow information to flow from one neuron to another. Northwestern scientists have found that without adequate kalirin, the frontal cortex of the brain of a person with schizophrenia only has a few narrow roads. The information from neurons gets jammed up like rush hour traffic on an interstate highway squeezed to a single lane.

"Without enough pathways, the information takes much longer to travel between neurons and much of it will never arrive," said Peter Penzes, assistant professor of physiology at the Feinberg School. He is senior author of a paper reporting the findings published in a recent issue [August 4, 2009] of the *Proceedings of the National Academy of Science*. Michael Cahill, a Feinberg doctoral student in neuroscience, is the lead author.

Penzes discovered the kalirin effect after he created the mouse model, which was the first to have a low level of kalirin and the first to develop symptoms of schizophrenia as an adolescent (two months old in mouse time). This mimics the delayed onset of the disease in humans. In normal development, the brain ramps up the production of kalirin as it begins to mature in adolescence.

"This discovery opens a new direction for treating the devastating cognitive symptoms of schizophrenia," Penzes

> **FAST FACT**
>
> Studies show that people with schizophrenia have a two- to threefold higher risk of dying compared with the general population.

Mice with Schizophrenic Behaviors Have Stunted Brain Pathways

Dendritic spines play an important role in carrying electrical signals in the brains of mice and humans. Studies of mice have found a connection between a reduced spine count per dendrite pathway and behaviors associated with human schizophrenics.

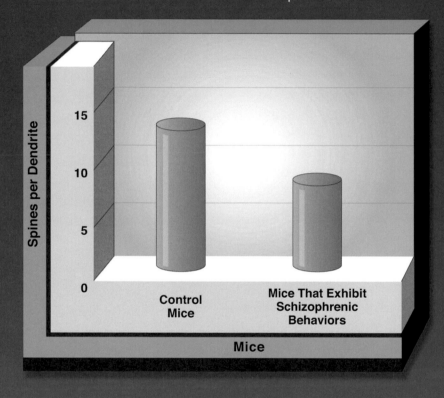

Taken from: A.V. Savonenko et al., "Alteration of BACE1 = Dependent NRG1/ErbB4 Signaling and Schizophrenia = Like Phenotypes in BACE1 = Null Mice," *Proceedings of the National Academy of Science*, April 8, 2008.

said. "There is currently no treatment for that. It suggests that if you can stimulate and amplify the activity of the protein kalirin that remains in the brain, perhaps we can help the symptoms."

Currently the only drug treatment for schizophrenia is an antipsychotic. "The drugs address the hallucinations and calm down the patient, but they don't improve their working memory (the ability of the brain to temporarily store and manage information required for complex mental tasks such as learning and reasoning) or their ability to think or their social behavior," Penzes said. "So you end up with patients who still can't integrate into society. Many attempt suicide."

Studies on Mouse Brains May Lead to a New Treatment

A few years ago in postmortem examinations of schizophrenic human brains, other scientists had found fewer connections between the brain cells in the frontal cortex and lower levels of kalirin. But the scientists couldn't show whether one condition led to the other.

With the new mouse model, Penzes was able to demonstrate that the low level of kalirin resulted in fewer dendritic spines in the frontal cortex of the brain, the part of the brain responsible for problem solving, planning and reasoning. Other areas of the brain had a normal number

Because the brains of humans and mice share many functional similarities, researchers have found schizophrenic mice to be particularly useful in the developing and testing of drugs for schizophrenia.
(AP Images)

of the dendritic spines. Human brains and mouse brains share many similarities in the way they function, Penzes said.

The new schizophrenic mouse model also exhibits more schizophrenic symptoms than other models, making these mice especially good for drug testing and development, Penzes said. The mice with low amounts of kalirin had a poor working memory, were antisocial and hyperactive.

Penzes said future studies would aim at enhancing the function of kalirin in the brain in an effort to correct the cognitive symptoms of schizophrenia.

People with Schizophrenia Deal with Stigma

Nadia Kadri and Norman Sartorius

In the following selection Nadia Kadri and Norman Sartorius contend that people suffering from schizophrenia face stigma in virtually every area of life—in school, at work, and even in family life. Kadri and Sartorius say that society has always stigmatized schizophrenia and other mental illnesses, but the negativity has become stronger in recent years. The authors discuss how an international program sponsored by the World Psychiatric Association is helping fight the stigma associated with schizophrenia. Kadri is the president of the Moroccan Society of Psychiatry. Sartorius is the scientific director of the World Psychiatric Association Global Programme against Stigma and Discrimination Because of Schizophrenia.

The stigma attached to mental illness is the greatest obstacle to the improvement of the lives of people with mental illness and their families. Such stigma results in (1) a lower priority for mental health services, (2) difficulty getting staff of good quality to work in these services, (3) continuing problems in finding employment and housing for people who have had an episode of mental disorder, (4) the social isolation of people who suffer from mental illness and their families, and (5) poorer quality of care for physical illnesses occurring in people diagnosed as having had psychiatric illnesses. These effects of stigma are true for all mental disorders, and in particular, for schizophrenia.

The history of the stigmatisation of mental illness is long, but it is probable that intolerance to mental abnormality (and the rejection of people who had it) has

Sources of Stigma

Percentage of schizophrenics who have felt stigmatized by the following groups of people:

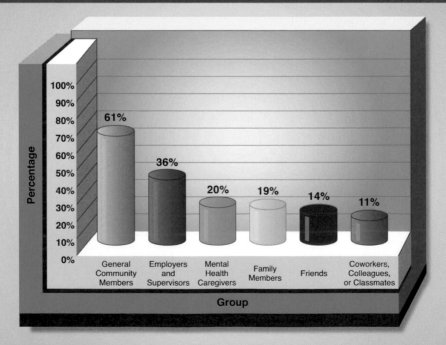

Taken from: Faith Dickerson et al., "Experiences of Stigma Among Outpatients with Schizophrenia," *Schizophrenia Bulletin*, vol. 128, no. 1, 2002, p. 149.

become stronger in the past two centuries because of urbanisation and the growing demands for skills and qualifications in almost all sectors of employment. This, however, is only part of the story: mental illness is also linked to stigmatisation, discrimination, and intolerance in rural settings and in all countries, regardless of their level of industrialisation and sophistication of labour. Recent studies carried out in developing countries confirm that this stigma is universal—indeed it is fair to say that stigma is attached to mental illness in different socio-cultural settings throughout the world, and that it is growing in strength and in its negative consequences.

Fighting Stigma with Collaborative Programmes

A number of programmes to diminish the stigma related to mental illness and its consequences have been started in recent years. Among those well known are campaigns undertaken in Australia, the United Kingdom [UK], and Sweden—for example, "Changing Minds," an anti-stigma campaign, was launched in 1998 by the United Kingdom Royal College of Psychiatrists. A major international effort is The Global Programme against Stigma and Discrimination Because of Schizophrenia, launched by the World Psychiatric Association (WPA) in 1996.

The WPA programme, known as "Open the Doors", has five important characteristics that distinguish it from other previously developed programmes. First, it is an international and collaborative programme. Second, it is conceived as a long-term programme rather than as a campaign. Third, it involves family and patient organisations as well as governments, community agents, and health services at all stages of the programme, from its planning to its evaluation. Fourth, it emphasises the need for sharing experience and information obtained in the course of the programmes among all concerned, within and between countries. Finally, and perhaps most importantly, the programme's targets are selected on the basis of a process of consultation with people who have schizophrenia and their families rather than on the basis of theoretical constructs. This means that the targets of the programmes in different countries (and even in different regions of the same country) vary. It also means that the forces uniting the programme are shared convictions about the principal and overall goals of the programme rather than an imposed and artificial uniformity of specific short-term objectives. The WPA programme has already involved some 18 countries as follows: Austria, Brazil, Canada, Chile, Egypt, Germany, Greece, India, Italy, Japan, Morocco, Poland, Romania, Slovakia, Spain, Turkey, the UK, and the United States. It is likely that other countries, for example Zambia and the Czech Republic as well as others, will join it in the years to come.

To reach the main goal of the programme—the reduction or elimination of stigma and its consequences—the participating sites have undertaken studies aimed at a better understanding of the causes of stigma, its mechanism of action, and the factors that increase or lessen it. Participating sites have also implemented an array of measures that were selected taking into account the country and its specificities.

Principles of Anti-Stigma Programmes

Work with patients and relatives. A central priority must be to boost patients' (and families') self-esteem and self-respect. This facilitates patients' socialisation, their active participation in the treatment and rehabilitation process, and their motivation for better personal care.

Work with members of the health professions. Emphasis has been placed on the fact that health workers can do a great deal (as individuals) to prevent or diminish stigmatisation by: (1) helping their patients maintain self-esteem, (2) developing and implementing the plan of treatment together, (3) being constantly aware of the

Norman Sartorius, pictured, is director of the World Psychiatric Association (WPA). He believes that the WPA program "Open the Doors" is successfully fighting the stigma associated with schizophrenia.
(AP Images)

danger of labelling, which might harm their patients, (4) ensuring that they have respected their patients' priorities rather then placing these priorities below those of the health care system, (5) working with families (learning from their experience and providing them with practical and useful information), and (6) in society, acting as advocates and models of tolerance and acceptance of people with mental illness.

Work with health authorities. Emphasis has been placed on the need to re-examine and improve legislation and procedures governing the health system to avoid its stigmatising potential.

Work with journalists and other media professionals. Journalists have been engaged in righting stigma through better reporting about mental illness and about people with mental illness. In Ireland and the Philippines, for example, journalists have been led by the anti-stigma programme to the formulation of a voluntary code of non-stigmatising reporting.

Work with the general public. The focus here has been on a change in behaviour rather than only a change of attitudes.

The sites participating in the programme are learning from each other through contacts, visits, and the exchange of information. In addition, the programme has identified certain strategic directives that have been incorporated into the rules for new programmes. On the basis of experience, the key documents of the programme—a step-by-step guide on programme development and the manual attached to it—are constantly updated and improved. . . .

Change Takes Time

The success of the WPA programme is evaluated at country level and with direct reference to the targets identified by patients and their families as being particularly important for them. This is being done by focus group explorations of the experiences patients and families have had since the programme in their country began. Surveys of attitudes before the programme and during its course have been done in some countries (e.g., Canada). In addition, there are general indications of the success of the programme, including the increasingly wide use of programme materials, continuing collaboration among the sites, the number of publications and requests for presentation of the programme by both professional and nonprofessional organisations. A detailed description of these matters and references to publications from the participating sites are being published.

The main obstacle to success is the fact that changes in attitudes and behaviour take time. Continuous repetition of action and financial support have to be maintained over years—despite the fact that, in the beginning, anti-stigma programmes often produce only meagre results. Maintaining the motivation of all concerned over many years is very difficult. The programme also needs the lasting involvement of all structures of the health system (and of other social services), which must see the fight against stigma as one of their permanent and essential tasks.

In the descriptions of work done in the sites participating in the WPA Global Programme against Stigma and Discrimination Because of Schizophrenia, there are many examples of actions that have contributed to the lessening of stigma or to the prevention of its consequences. These examples underline the three basic principles that should be kept in mind when fighting stigma.

First, the fight against stigma is a priority because stigmatisation is a major obstacle to any progress in the field of mental health. Second, programmes against stigma and discrimination should select their targets and evaluate their success with the active and concrete involvement of people with mental illness and their families. Finally, each of us, whether part of a major programme or alone, can do something to diminish or avoid stigmatisation by mental illness. It is just as important to ask what we can do ourselves to diminish stigmatisation as it is to urge others to do something about it.

> **FAST FACT**
>
> According to Suicide .org, 10 percent of people who have schizophrenia commit suicide.

CHAPTER 2

Issues and Controversies
Concerning Schizophrenia

Schizophrenia Is a Medical Disease

Rashmi Nemade and Mark Dombeck

In the following article Rashimi Nemade and Mark Dombeck contend that schizophrenia is a biologically based brain disease. According to Nemade and Dombeck, scientists have found structural, biochemical, and functional differences between schizophrenic brains and normal brains. The authors say that taken as a whole, the available scientific evidence supports the contention that schizophrenia is a medical disease. Nemade is a contributing writer and Dombeck is the director of Mental Help Net, an online resource for mental health information and education.

D ata from modern scientific research prove that schizophrenia is unequivocally a biological disease of the brain, just like Alzheimer's Disease and Bipolar Disorder. For one thing, schizophrenia is now known to be partially caused by genetics and to be inherited. For another, modern non-invasive brain

SOURCE: Rashmi Nemade and Mark Dombeck, "Evidence That Schizophrenia Is a Brain Disease," Mentalhelp.net, February 14, 2006. Copyright © CenterSite, LLC. Reproduced by permission, www.mentalhelp.net.

Photo on facing page. Many controversies surround the diagnosis and treatment of schizophrenia. (Tim Vernon, LTH NHS Trust/ Photo Researchers, Inc.)

imaging techniques such as Magnetic Resonance Imaging (MRI) and Computerized Tomography (CT), have documented structural differences between schizophrenic and normal brains. Individuals with schizophrenia have up to 25% less volume of gray matter in their brains, especially in the temporal and frontal lobes (known to be important for coordination of thinking and judgment). Patients demonstrating the worst brain tissue losses also tend to show the worst symptoms.

Schizophrenic Brains Are Different

Functional scanning of the brain, using technologies like Positron Emission Tomography (PET) and functional MRI have made it possible to create real-time maps of regional cerebral blood flow and metabolism, providing another window into how schizophrenic brains are distinct from normal brains. Such studies tend to show low levels of activation in schizophrenic patients' middle frontal cortex and inferior parietal cortex compared to normal people included as control subjects. Low activity findings like this are also correlated with (related to) increased negative symptoms (meaning that people who tend to have more negative symptoms, also tend to show lower levels of brain activity in key brain areas).

Schizophrenic brains are thus (on average) different in terms of total tissue volume, and activity. However, there is most often no obvious single point of structural damage (a "lesion") to point at as the specific location in the brain where schizophrenia is happening.

In addition to structural differences, schizophrenic brains also show neurochemical differences when compared with normal brains. The brain uses a number of chemical messengers, called neurotransmitters, to communicate among its millions of individual neurons. At the most basic level, schizophrenic brains appear to be differentially sensitive to the neurotransmitter dopamine

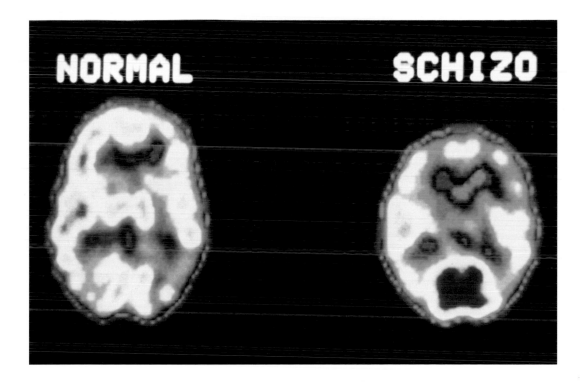

NORMAL SCHIZO

compared to normal brains. The "dopamine hypothesis" of schizophrenia holds that schizophrenia is caused by excess dopamine (or excessive sensitivity to dopamine). Support for this hypothesis comes from several main sources. First, drugs known to block the effects of dopamine in the brain are also known to be useful as antipsychotic medications (they reduce the intensity and frequency of hallucinations, for example). Second, stimulant drugs like cocaine and methamphetamine, which are known to either mimic the action of dopamine, or to cause dopamine to become more active in the brain, are known to be capable of causing hallucinations and delusions in non-schizophrenic people (if enough of those substances are taken). It is also known that too little dopamine is responsible for Parkinson's disease, and that chronic use of antipsychotic medications (which block dopamine) can result in a Parkinson's-like condition called tardive dyskinesia.

An imaging technique known as positron emission tomography makes it possible to see how schizophrenic brains differ from normal brains.
(Science Source/Photo Researchers, Inc.)

While the dopamine hypothesis has been dominant for a long time, it has taken a research beating in recent years, and it is no longer so clear that dopamine alone is responsible for causing schizophrenia. Today, it appears more likely that other neurotransmitters are involved in creating conditions for schizophrenia and psychosis, including serotonin (implicated in depression and anxiety), and glutamate (which is known to be implicated in the hallucinatory effects of the drug PCP ("angel dust")). Though the details of neurochemical involvement in schizophrenia change as new findings accumulate, the essential neurochemical basis of schizophrenia has been quite firmly established and would now appear to be beyond question.

Functional Deficits

Considered as a group and compared to normal people, schizophrenics show observable functional deficits as well. Functional deficits are problems people have in performing basic mental and physical tasks and activities such as remembering things, using executive functioning (being able to flexibly shift between various tasks, making judgment, etc.), intuiting rules from consequences, and hand grip strength. On average, schizophrenic people show reduced memory, attention span, executive functioning, and reaction time compared to normal people. They have relatively more difficulty recalling things they learned five minutes before than normal people, for example, but are equally able to recall long-term memories. They tend to be more distractable and have a harder time engaging in problem solving and planning efforts than do normal people.

Abnormalities in sensory processing are also evident in schizophrenic patients. It is common for schizophrenic patients to show "soft" neurological signs, meaning that

FAST FACT

According to a survey by the National Alliance on Mental Illness, 85 percent of people believe that schizophrenia is a medical illness.

Schizophrenic Brains Are Out of Sync

Studies have shown that while performing a straightforward task, schizophrenic brains are more active and irregular than healthy brains, though both groups perform equally well.

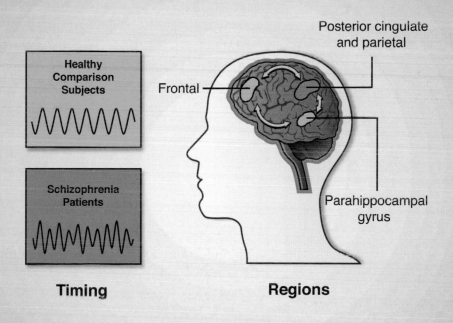

Timing

Regions

Taken from: Schizophrenia Daily News Blog, "In Schizophrenia, Brain's Default Mode Seems to Be Out of Sync," March 14, 2007. www.schizophronia.com.

they might have difficulty distinguishing between two simultaneous touches or in being able to identify numbers drawn on the palm of their hand. They also tend to confuse the right and left sides of their bodies more frequently than normal people. Such well documented observations of sensory processing problems suggest impairments or irregularities in the way that schizophrenics' brains are wired.

Still more evidence of neurological impairment in schizophrenia comes from consideration of electroencephalogram (EEG) data, which are tests of brain electrical activity. About one-third of schizophrenic people show abnormal electrical brain impulses, also suggesting irregularities in the way schizophrenic brains are wired.

Considered as a whole, these numerous and methodologically distinct results suggest converging and compelling evidence for the idea that schizophrenia is basically a biologically based brain disease.

Mental Illnesses Are Not Medical Diseases

Thomas Szasz

In the following viewpoint Thomas Szasz contends that schizophrenia and other mental illnesses are not medical diseases. According to Szasz, the view that mental illness is a medical disease is based on a dubious history. Additionally, this history is laden with examples of cruel "treatments" that infringed on the rights of those labeled as mentally ill. Szasz questions the practice of medicine on mental health patients with no evidence of medical disease. Szasz is a professor emeritus of psychiatry at the State University of New York Health Science Center in Syracuse. He is also the author of several books, including *The Myth of Mental Illness* and *Schizophrenia: The Sacred Symbol of Psychiatry*.

A 1999 White House Conference on Mental Health concluded: "Research in the last decade proves that mental illnesses are diagnosable disorders of the brain." President William Clinton was more specific: "Mental illness can be accurately diagnosed, successfully treated, just as physical illness." Persons who reject the view that mental illnesses are physical diseases are dismissed by today's opinion-makers as intellectual troglodytes, on a par with "flatearthers."

The Assumption of True Mental Disease

That the claim that "mental illnesses are diagnosable disorders of the brain" is a lie ought to be evident to anyone who thinks for himself. Here I want to show that the claim that "research in the last decade proves [this]" is also a lie, one more in a very long list in the history of

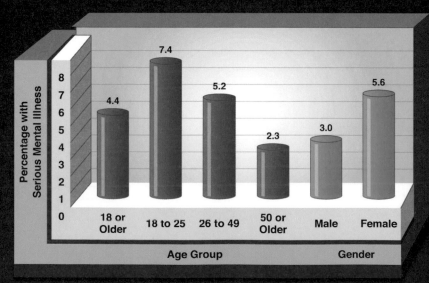

The Prevalence of Serious Mental Illness in the United States, 2008

The U.S. Department of Health and Human Services defines persons with serious mental illness as those "who currently or at any time in the past year have had a diagnosable mental, behavioral, or emotional disorder . . . that has resulted in serious functional impairment, which substantially interferes with or limits one or more major life activities."

Percentage with Serious Mental Illness

Age Group				Gender	
18 or Older	18 to 25	26 to 49	50 or Older	Male	Female
4.4	7.4	5.2	2.3	3.0	5.6

Taken from: U.S. Department of Health and Human Services, "Results from the 2008 National Survey on Drug Use and Health: National Findings," September 10, 2009.

psychiatry. The contention that mental illness is brain disease is as old as psychiatry itself: it is an integral part of the grand lie that psychiatry is a branch of medicine and healing, when in fact it is a branch of the law and social control. [Political theorist] Hannah Arendt was right when she observed: "There are no limits to the possibilities of nonsense and capricious notions that can be decked out as the last word in science."

The idea that mental illness is a bodily disease dates back to the premodern medical conception of disease as "humoral imbalance," comically prefiguring the modern, supposedly scientific conception of it as "chemical imbalance." In the United States, the idea of mental illness as humoral imbalance was famously espoused by Benjamin Rush (1746–1813), the founding father of American psychiatry. Rush did not discover that certain behaviors are diseases; he decreed that they are: "Lying," he declared, "is a corporeal disease." In a letter to his friend John Adams, he wrote: "The subjects [mental diseases] have hitherto been enveloped in mystery. I have endeavored to bring them down to the level of all other diseases of the human body, and to show that the mind and the body are moved by the same causes and subject to the same laws."

The Development of Psychiatry

In the nineteenth century the scientific concept of disease as lesion replaced the Galenic concept of disease as humoral imbalance. Now, physicians postulated that mental diseases are diseases of the brain. From about 1850 until past World War I, German (more precisely, German-speaking) psychiatry ruled the field. The very term psychiatry (*Psychiatrie*) was a German invention, coined in 1808 by Johann Christian Reil (1759–1813). Reil, not an alienist (psychiatrist), was one of the outstanding medical scientists and physicians of his age. He was a friend and physician of Johann Wolfgang von Goethe. In addition to coining the term "psychiatry," he also coined the term "noninjurious torture," to describe the methods of frightening mental patients that he considered effective and legitimate "treatments."

It is important to keep in mind that the German asylum system was created, in 1805, by the autocratic Prussian state: specifically, by Karl August von Hardenberg (1759–1822), a Prussian statesman. Hardenberg declared, "The state must concern itself with all institutions *for those with damaged minds*, both for the betterment of the unfortunates and the advancement of science. In this important and difficult *field of medicine* only unrelenting efforts will enable us to carve out advances for the good of suffering mankind. Perfection can be achieved only in such institutions."

Writing in 1917, at the height of World War I, Emil Kraepelin (1856–1926)—creator of the first system of psychiatric classification, today widely considered the father of modern "scientific" psychiatry—offered these revealing remarks about Hardenberg's achievement: "The great war in which we are now engaged has compelled us to recognize the fact that science could forge for us a host of effective weapons for use against a hostile world. Should it be otherwise if we are fighting an internal enemy seeking to destroy the very fabric of our existence?"

Kraepelin's remarks make clear that he regarded psychiatry as an arm of the state, similar to the military forces, whose duty is to protect the fatherland from "an internal enemy" that, like a hostile army, seeks to destroy it. The evil genius of psychiatry lay, and continues to lie, in its ability to convince itself, the legal system, and the public that, in matters defined as psychiatric, there is no conflict between the legitimate interests of the individual and the legitimate interests of the political class in charge of the state.

Of course, the German psychiatric pioneers had to answer the question, "What is mental illness?" Answer

German psychiatrist Emil Kraepelin was the creator of the first system of psychiatric classification and is considered the father of modern "scientific" psychiatry. (Hulton Archive/Getty Images)

it they did. Wilhelm Griesinger (1817–1868), considered one of the founders of German psychiatry— and also of the famed Zurich insane asylum, the *Burghölzli*— declared: "Psychological diseases are diseases of the brain. . . . Insanity is merely a symptom complex of various anomalous states of the brain."

Theodor Meynert (1833–1892)—a German-born Viennese neuropsychiatrist and one of [neurologist and psychoanalyst Sigmund] Freud's teachers—began his textbook, *Psychiatry* (1884), with this statement: "The reader will find no other definition of 'Psychiatry' in this book but the one given on the title page: *Clinical Treatise on Diseases of the Forebrain*. The historical term for psychiatry, i.e., 'treatment of the soul,' implies more than we can accomplish, and transcends the bounds of accurate scientific investigation."

In a review of Swedish psychiatry in the nineteenth century, historian of science Roger Qvarsell states: "In the 1860s, the debate among psychiatrists about the real nature of mental disease was over. . . . Almost all medical scientists and medical authorities were at this time convinced that mental diseases were of the same nature as somatic disorders." . . .

Infringement of Freedom

What inferences did and do doctors draw from their concepts of mental illness as brain disease? First, as Carl Wernicke (1848–1905), a prominent nineteenth-century German neuropsychiatrist observed, "The medical treatment of [mental] patients began with the infringement of their personal freedom." In addition, it began with "benevolent tortures," such as frightening them by throwing them into a pit of snakes, the origin of the term "snake pit" for insane asylum. More specifically, the humoral-imbalance theory led Rush to employ "bleeding, purging, low diet, and the tranquilizing chair." The tranquilizing chair was a chair-like contraption for confining the patient and rotating him until he became dizzy or lost consciousness. This was supposed to rebalance the circulation in the brain. It was but a small step from the nineteenth century's tranquilizing chair to the twentieth century's tranquilizing drug, supposed to rebalance the chemical imbalance in the patient's brain.

Psychiatric practice today requires that doctors and patients ignore evidence and be ignorant of history. There was no evidence for a humoral imbalance causing illness, but the doctrine prevailed for two thousand years. There is no evidence for a chemical imbal-

> **FAST FACT**
>
> According to the National Institute of Mental Health, an estimated 26.2 percent of Americans aged eighteen and older suffer from a diagnosable mental disorder in a given year.

ance causing mental illness, but that does not impair the doctrine's scientific standing or popularity. Neither the American Psychiatric Association nor American presidents remind people of the caveat of the great nineteenth-century English neurologist John Hughlings Jackson (1835–1911): "Our concern as medical men is with the body. If there be such a thing as disease of the mind, we can do nothing for it."

The Term "Schizophrenia" Should Be Changed

Patricia Jane Teskey

In the following article Patricia Jane Teskey asserts that the name "schizophrenia" should be changed because it does not appropriately convey the biological basis of the disease, and it is stigmatizing. Teskey says the term "schizophrenia" inappropriately conjures up scary images of Dr. Jekyll and Mr. Hyde and other fictional split personalities, which do not convey the true nature of the disease. She thinks the label "schizophrenia" should be dropped and a more appropriate, less stigmatizing name should be used. Teskey is a writer based in Toronto, Canada.

"The stigma will never disappear," mused one father, "until we change the name of this illness." Our support group for family caregivers of people with schizophrenia was almost over. Around the circle, we had told our stories. We were struck by the fact that more than half of us were unable to help our ill

SOURCE: Patricia Jane Teskey, "What's in a Name? A Case for Changing the 'S' Word," *Schizophrenia Digest*, Spring 2006, pp. 30–31. Reproduced by permission.

relatives to reach their full potential because of their un-willingness to accept professional help.

"Schizophrenia" is a scary word. People on the receiving end of this diagnosis cringe and deny, and they are not alone. Have you noticed how we family supporters can talk about this illness for hours without saying its name? We are adept at avoiding the "s" word.

Schizophrenia's Negative Connotations

This dad, then, made a thought-provoking observation. A rose by any other name might smell the same. But, would schizophrenia by some other name be, well, maybe a whole lot better understood, more accepted, and less stigmatized?

Stigma cannot be reduced to a single cause. But, can a name starting with "schizo" meaning "split" ever lose its negative connotations? Will it ever be rid of the 'split personality' misperception? Perhaps we have a responsibility to ask ourselves this question.

Some educational materials explain that schizophrenia means a "split from reality" or a "splitting of the various parts of the thought process." These may (or may not) be good translations from the Greek; but three things are certain: the name "schizophrenia" fails to communicate the biological nature of this illness; it contributes to fear and denial in people diagnosed with it; and it evokes negative attitudes toward them by the general public.

Historically, the term "schizophrenia" has always been misunderstood. Coined by Swiss psychiatrist Eugen Bleuler, and accepted for use in 1911, it immediately became associated in the public imagination with Robert Louis Stevenson's *The Strange Case of Dr. Jekyll and Mr. Hyde*, an 1886 gothic novel about a doctor who is kind and pleasant by day, but a murderer by night. Consequently, for nearly 100 years, fictional books and movies have continued to depict people with schizophrenia as having violent, "split" (dual or multiple) personalities.

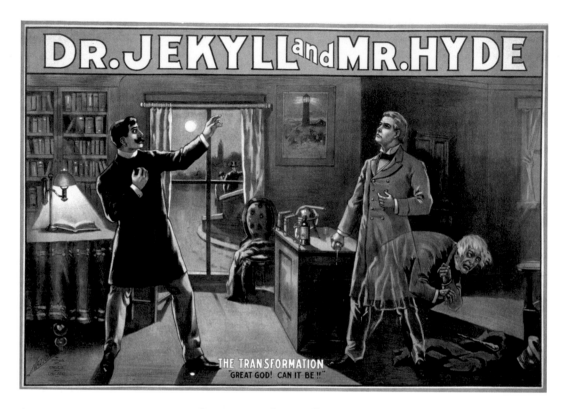

Schizophrenia began being stereotyped when it became associated in the public imagination with Robert Louis Stevenson's 1886 novel *The Strange Case of Dr. Jekyll and Mr. Hyde,* an illustration from which is shown here. (APIC/ Getty Images)

Can we realistically expect to control how "schizophrenia" and "schizophrenic" are used? The most that advocates can do, advises a senior editor at Merriam-Webster's Incorporated, is to persuade dictionary editors that the second usage is offensive to a specific group of people. If so persuaded, the editors will include this in the next edition. Indeed, some ground has been gained here: *Encarta Webster's Dictionary of the English Language,* 2004 edition, has a second definition for "schizophrenia" as "an *offensive* term for a state characterized by contradictory or conflicting attitudes, behavior, or qualities *(insult)*." (Italics mine.) *Canadian Oxford Dictionary's* 2005 edition concurs, though tentatively: "Some people feel that using 'schizophrenia' and 'schizophrenic' in reference to mere contradiction or inconsistency makes light of what is a serious disease."

The basic point, explains Bob Carolla, director of media relations for NAMI (National Alliance on Mental Illness) and supervisor of its StigmaBusters program, "is 'people first' language. You don't define a person by their illness; so, don't use an adjective as a noun, as in 'a schizophrenic.'" Yet, in spite of our advocacy, this reductive labelling continues to be a persistent, stubborn source of dehumanization and stigma.

Are we wasting our precious resources fighting it? Would it be better to abandon the term "schizophrenia"

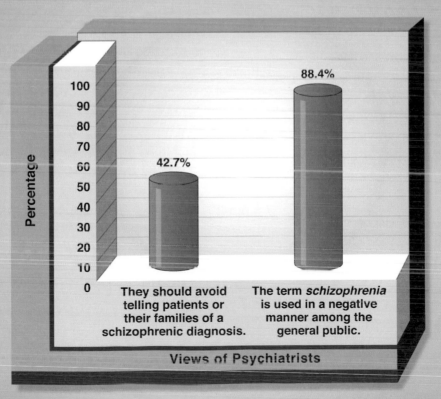

Taken from: Alp Üçok et al., "Attitudes of Psychiatrists Toward Patients with Schizophrenia," *Psychiatry and Clinical Neurosciences*, December 17, 2003.

and rename this illness? Should we take a leaf from the book of the AIDS community? The name AIDS spells out in plain English exactly what it is: Acquired Immune Deficiency Syndrome. No room for myth or misperception there. Anyone not knowing the meaning of these words can find clear, accurate definitions in any dictionary.

Call It Mind-Split Disease

What new name could we give schizophrenia? One possibility was used by researchers Ka Fai Chung and John Hung Chan from the department of psychiatry, University of Hong Kong, China, who surveyed high school students in Hong Kong to test if attitudes toward people with schizophrenia would improve with a less pejorative, more clinical/biological name. Some students saw the illness named "mind-split disease" (as schizophrenia is translated in China), while others saw "Dysfunction of thought and perception." (As it happens, attitudes did not measurably improve with the second name, but the authors conclude that the sample was too small and more research is needed.)

Officially, any new name must be chosen by committees of experts who refine and revise the *Diagnostic and Statistical Manual of Mental Disorders (DSM)* published by the American Psychiatric Association (APA). Standards for changing the name of a disorder are different than those for revising criteria. An integral part of the overall revision process is intensive scientific research literature reviews and new data analyses, which form the scientific basis for the changes made.

The next *DSM (DSM-V)* is slated for publication in 2011— exactly 100 years since this illness received its present name. Before beginning formal work on it later in 2006, the APA is inviting *DSM* users—the public and professional—to rename the disorder. . . . "Theoreti-

FAST FACT

Seventy-two percent of people with schizophrenia conceal their diagnosis, according to a survey of hundreds of people with schizophrenia from twenty-seven countries.

cally, there is a possibility that the name would change," advises William E. Narrow, MD, Associate Director, Division of Research, at the APA. "However, no one has made such a suggestion to the *DSM* staff in recent years."

What do *you* think? Is it time to suggest a name change for schizophrenia?

The Term "Schizophrenia" Should Not Be Changed

Jeffrey A. Lieberman and Michael B. First

In the following article Jeffrey A. Lieberman and Michael B. First contend that schizophrenia is a valid diagnostic classification and that its name should not be changed. According to Lieberman and First, the label "schizophrenia" is medically and scientifically useful in describing a pattern of symptoms including delusions, hallucinations, and catatonic behavior. The authors think that changing the name of the disease will not quell the public's fear and ignorance of schizophrenia and other mental disorders. Lieberman is chairman of the Department of Psychiatry at the College of Physicians and Surgeons of Columbia University. First is a professor of clinical psychiatry at Columbia University.

Recent reports in the media have called for schizophrenia to be "abolished as a concept" because it is scientifically meaningless. This is not the first time that the validity of this diagnostic en-

SOURCE: Jeffrey A Lieberman and Michael B. First, "Renaming Schizophrenia," *British Medical Journal*, vol. 334, January 20, 2007, p. 48. Copyright © 2007 British Medical Association. Reproduced by permission of BMJ Publishing Group, conveyed through Copyright Clearance Center, Inc.

tity has been challenged, and it will not be the last until the cause of the disorder and its precise pathophysiology are known.

The current system of psychiatric diagnosis cannot describe definitive disease entities because of our inability to demonstrate "natural" boundaries between disorders. However, as [psychiatrists Robert] Kendell and [Assen] Jablensky point out, "thoughtful clinicians have long been aware that diagnostic categories are simply concepts, justified only by whether they provide a useful framework for organising and explaining the complexity of clinical experience in order to derive inferences about outcome and to guide decisions about treatment." In this context, the charge that schizophrenia does not define a specific illness is clearly unwarranted. Although the validity of the diagnosis remains to be established, its diagnostic reliability and usefulness are indisputable.

A Valid Diagnosis

For more than 100 years schizophrenia has been an integral part of our nosology [disease classification] and has facilitated research and treatment of people affected by this disease. People qualify for the diagnosis if their clinical signs and symptoms conform to the operational diagnostic criteria that define schizophrenia. Many studies have shown that these diagnostic criteria can be applied reliably and accurately by trained mental health professionals. Although a diagnosis of schizophrenia depends on the presence of a pattern of symptoms (such as delusions, hallucinations, disorganised speech, disorganized or catatonic behaviour, and negative symptoms such as lack of motivation), evidence shows that these are manifestations of brain pathology. Schizophrenia is not caused by disturbed psychological development or

> **FAST FACT**
>
> According to the World Health Organization, schizophrenia affects males and females equally, although symptoms often appear earlier in males.

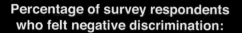

People with Schizophrenia Experience Discrimination

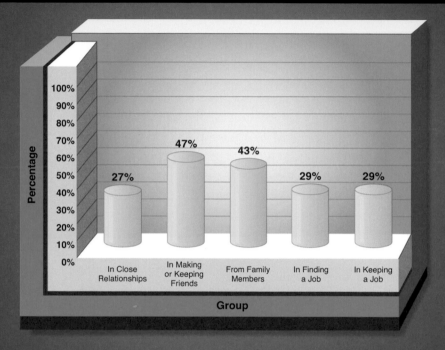

Percentage of survey respondents who felt negative discrimination:

Taken from: Graham Thornicroft et al., *Lancet*, "Global Study Shows People with Schizophrenia Both Expect and Experience Discrimination, January 2009.

bad parenting. Compared with normal controls, people with schizophrenia have abnormalities in brain structure and function seen on neuroimaging and electrophysiological tests. In addition, the evidence that vulnerability to schizophrenia is at least partly genetic is indisputable.

Once a diagnosis of schizophrenia is made, the treating clinician has a wide array of treatment options available, which have been tested empirically on similar groups of people. Furthermore, the doctor will also have access to the huge body of empirical data that characterises this condition including its course, treatment response, outcome, and family history. This is important because evidence shows that early intervention may improve outcome. The diagnosis also helps when explaining to the patient and their family the nature of the problem, the range of treatments and outcomes, and the assistance available from support groups.

Of course, diagnostic labels have potential disadvantages. If a diagnosis of schizophrenia is mistakenly applied, the patient will receive the wrong treatment and potentially have the stigma of having a mental illness. For example, if a patient with a toxic (such as phencyclidine induced) psychosis is misdiagnosed with schizophrenia, he or she may be given a long and unnecessary course of antipsychotic drugs. To avoid this situation, psychiatric diagnoses have built-in safeguards in the form of exclusion criteria that prevent a diagnosis from being made if certain conditions are present(for example, a diagnosis of schizophrenia is not permitted unless psychotic symptoms persist for a substantial period of time after the person has stopped using the drug in question).

The Stigma Will Not Disappear

Concerns about potential stigma associated with having a serious mental illness have resulted in proposals to change the name of schizophrenia. "Integration disorder" and "dopamine dysregulation disorder" have been suggested as possible alternatives. Unfortunately, changing the name of the condition (or even abolishing the concept) will not affect the root cause of the stigma—the public's ignorance and fear of people with mental illness. Renaming may even have the unintended effect that the person, rather than the illness, is blamed for the symptoms. Ultimately, we must gain a more complete understanding of the causes and pathophysiological

Some people advocate changing the term "schizophrenia" to diminish the stigma attached to the disorder and to lessen the public's ignorance about and fear of mental illness. Mental health advocates argue that changing the name of the illness will not eliminate these problems. **(David Gifford/Photo Researchers, Inc.)**

mechanisms underlying schizophrenia. Only then can we replace the way we characterise schizophrenia with a diagnosis that more closely conforms to a specific brain disease. In the meantime, we can be confident and grateful that the benefits conferred by the concept of schizophrenia far outweigh any perceived disadvantages.

Involuntary Treatment Laws Are Necessary

Bob Manhard

In the following viewpoint Bob Manhard argues that involuntary treatment laws are necessary to protect schizophrenics and other severely mentally ill people from making bad decisions. Manhard says his daughter suffers from schizophrenia and is unable to make rational and wise decisions. Because of this she refuses treatment, which could help her, and instead she lives a tragic, devastated life. Manhard argues that involuntary treatment laws are needed because his daughter and other severely mentally ill persons who refuse treatment are not acting in their best interests or those of society. Manhard is a member of the Colorado chapter of the National Alliance on Mental Illness (NAMI).

We who have been advocating for a change in our state laws which would provide for a new standard enabling an easier path for the involuntary commitment of nonviolent, but not "gravely" disabled, persons afflicted with a Neurobiological Brain

SOURCE: Bob Manhard, "Are Those with NBD Really 'Free to Choose?'" Treatment Advocacy Center, 2009. Copyright © 2009 Treatment Advocacy Center. Reproduced by permission.

Disease (NBD)—schizophrenia, bipolar, etc.—have all heard some pretty "far out" rationalizations from those who prefer the status quo and value preserving "civil rights" over protecting the health of mentally ill citizens.

Recently someone said to me, "Who are you to be thinking about bringing proceedings to force your mentally ill daughter to take medications. Your daughter is an adult, and she should be free to decide how she wants to live her life—including whether she wants to be involved in a treatment program. If the life she has chosen doesn't meet your wishes, that's something which you need to deal with because it should be her choice. Let her seek treatment when she is ready." This person implied that I was a controlling father who couldn't let go and wanted to direct my daughter's life indefinitely.

Severely Mentally Ill Persons Are Unable to Make Wise Decisions

Wow! This admonishment temporarily shook me and caused me to reflect as to whether she might have a point. . . . Then it dawned on me that she and a number of like-minded people assume that those with a severe mental illness have the "mental capacity" to make wise decisions about the state of their mental health, their need for treatment, and a whole host of other issues critical to their well being. But is that a valid assumption?

I am convinced that my daughter (call her Jane) wouldn't have "chosen" the life she is enduring if she was "free" to make wise choices. I have 3 other grown children (none afflicted with NBD) whose "life choices" have had the fortune to have the mental capacity which has led them to choose normal, happy, productive, lives.

Because some mentally ill people refuse to take medications, the author argues that involuntary treatment laws are needed. (BSIP/Photo Researchers, Inc.)

Those who assume that the severely mentally ill have sufficient insight into their mental condition also believe that they have often made "deliberate decisions" to live a confused, wretched life. These same naive people who talk about preserving "free choice" for those ill don't understand that to have "free choice" a person has to possess reasonable cognitive ability. Those with NBD simply don't have it!

If Jane was not seriously impaired from the effects of a severe brain disease called schizophrenia she would not have chosen the tragic life described below:

1. She is not capable of protecting herself from harm and was raped several years ago resulting in pregnancy.
2. She is in a constant state of mental confusion, frustration, and often fear. She is often highly paranoid and frequently hears voices. Jane knows that she is "slow" and finds it difficult to grasp the content of printed and verbal communications.
3. Her social life is nil. . . . She shuns old friends and is suspicious of everyone.
4. She agonizes over not having a job. She has been hired for approximately 25 jobs over the past 6 years but has lost them all because of distracting paranoia.
5. She lost custody of her two oldest children because after she left her mother's home [she] was unable to secure living accommodations for her children.
6. Jane has lost custody of two more babies in the past 3 years. Although she loves the children, she has difficulty relating to them and grows apart from them because of her inability to communicate well. Her fear of taking meds trumps her desire to regain custody.
7. Jane lives in a sub-poverty, one-room, flat with a "live-in" boyfriend. In a recent phone conversation, she alluded to having sex with him and one of his friends on a regular basis. Jane's illness causes her to fear using "protection" and I fear that it won't be long before she gives birth to another baby. No problem!!! The citizens of the state of Illinois will be more than happy to foot the bill for the birth and ongoing upkeep of the 5th child.

So who in their "right mind" would choose Jane's devastating life style?

Treating the mentally ill provides them with the opportunity to become functional and regain the cognitive ability that allows them to truly be "free" to choose wisely.

Involuntary Treatment Protects the Mentally Ill

State laws provide that when our children have reached legal age they're permitted to make decisions for themselves. Wisely, our society does not allow our youth to make their own important decisions—or to fend for themselves—before they reach "majority." Why? It takes

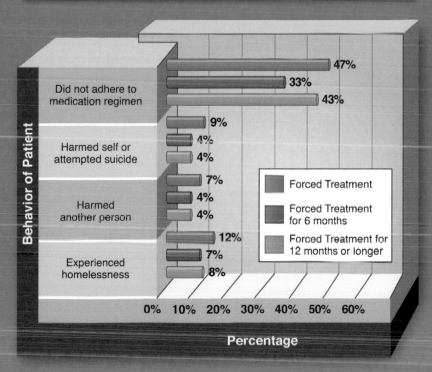

The Impact of New York's Involuntary Treatment Laws, 1999–2007

Behavior of Patient

Did not adhere to medication regimen: 47%, 33%, 43%

Harmed self or attempted suicide: 9%, 4%, 4%

Harmed another person: 7%, 4%, 4%

Experienced homelessness: 12%, 7%, 8%

Forced Treatment
Forced Treatment for 6 months
Forced Treatment for 12 months or longer

Percentage: 0% 10% 20% 30% 40% 50% 60%

Taken from: M.S. Swartz et al., "New York State Assisted Outpatient Treatment Program Evaluation," Duke University School of Medicine, June 2009.

years for the mind to develop through experience and knowledge to acquire reasonably "good judgment."

However, the vast majority of 12-year-olds are capable of making better choices than my 35-year-old daughter.

A most glaring contradiction. Most state laws call for protection of our mentally "immature" youth from any harmful results of their major decisions by allowing their loved ones to make those decisions (including medical decisions) for them. . . . But other laws in most states fail to protect Jane and other adult "mentally impaired" from decisions they make—thus allowing Jane and over a million other severely mentally ill to be trapped in their disease—to continue to be at great risk of unintended harm such as suicide, violence to themselves and others, homelessness, being wrongly jailed, and to degrading health and quality of life. . . .

Those with NBD, because of their mental impairment, aren't really "free" to make wise choices. Thus, state laws which continue to provide the right (for those who "lack insight" as to their illness) to refuse treatment are not in the best interest of that person nor society.

I've asked many who oppose changes to involuntary treatment laws—"then what solution do you have to offer to extricate the Janes of this world from their disease?" But they become silent when it comes to having alternative viable solutions.

Involuntary Treatment Laws Are Wrong

Aubrey Ellen Shomo

In the following article Aubrey Ellen Shomo says mental patients should not be forced to take mind-numbing medications to treat their disease. Shomo—who describes herself as a noncompliant mental patient—says mentally ill people should have the right, just as other patients do, to refuse treatment. According to Shomo, many noncompliant mental patients—herself included—have recovered, despite the medical community's assertion that they will be doomed to a tragic life without their medications. Shomo is a published author and recovering psychiatric patient.

I see it everywhere: People with mental illness need medication. It sounds reasonable. Today, there are even political organizations that seek to make it easy to force a person to take it.

It's easy to look at another and assume things like that. It's human. After all, it's compassionate to help someone

SOURCE: Aubrey Ellen Shomo, "The Manifesto of a Noncompliant Mental Patient," *Open Minds Quarterly*, Spring 2007. Copyright © 2007 Aubrey Ellen Shomo. Reproduced by permission of the author.

who isn't able to ask for help, right? They'll thank you in the long run, won't they?

No one asks why their child, or sibling or friend refuses to take their meds. Why bother? It's an illness. It's meaningless. The doctors say so. They know these things.

Have you ever questioned the logic of the phrase "She wouldn't be refusing medication if she wasn't ill"?

I am a noncompliant mental patient. I have been for years. I beg you. Ask why.

Why I Do Not Want Treatment

Look into my eyes and see me. Try to understand where I'm coming from. Even a crazy person has a human will. I am someone's sibling, someone's child, and someone's friend. I could be yours.

> **FAST FACT**
>
> According to the Treatment Advocacy Center, there are approximately 1.8 million Americans with untreated severe mental illness.

I've been told more times than I can count that I won't make it without medication. I've been told that I have a chemical imbalance. My brain's broken. I need it.

If I refuse, it's the side effects. They can treat them with more medication. If it isn't that, I lack insight. I don't know I'm sick.

Why would I possibly want to stop? How could I wish to do so? Let me ask you: Have you ever taken these drugs? They call it antipsychotic medication. It sounds good enough, but did you know these drugs are also called major tranquilizers?

They speak of side effects, but do you know what it feels like to have them? Can you read that on the label? On my label?

What's that? You learned all about this in medical school? Can you learn what it is to be in love from reading a medical description? Heart rate, neurotransmitters, behavior patterns. Three criteria out of five.

Can human experience be described in such simple terms? I bet you don't think yours can. Why, then, do you insist on describing mine? I know how major tranquilizers feel. I've had to.

They change a person. The vigor of human experience fades to shades of gray. Life becomes dull, boring, long. Creativity slips into nothingness. The very human spirit is dulled. You can go from the rapture of being alive to wondering if you even are.

They will make you calm. They will make you behave. They might even help with your problems, but they can dampen what really matters—what makes you alive. They majorly tranquilize.

"She prefers her mania—her madness. It's a symptom of the disease." How can you say what matters to me? Is that your right?

For this broken mind of mine, I have been locked up. I have been threatened. I have been restrained. I have suffered at the hands of a system I'm told is helping me. And they wonder why I don't trust them. How could I be hesitant, even bitter?

Some mental patients refuse to take medications, maintaining that their tranquilizing effects stifle creativity and dull the liveliness of the human spirit. (**SPL/ Photo Researchers, Inc.**)

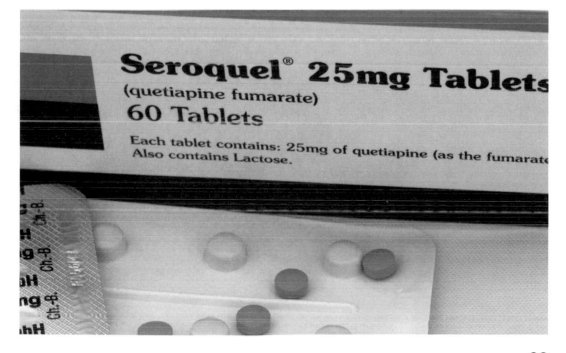

Seroquel® 25mg Tablets

(quetiapine fumarate)

60 Tablets

Each tablet contains: 25mg of quetiapine (as the fumarate
Also contains Lactose.

"She's paranoid. She won't take her medication." They might be right, but all I ever wanted is to make my own choices. I've only wanted to scream, "What about how I feel?!"

I am a noncompliant mental patient. Hear my voice.

Other Patients Have the Right to Refuse

A cancer patient can refuse chemotherapy. A religious person can choose to trust God over penicillin. A doctor would call both irrational, but acquiesce. All I ask is the same right.

"She'll decompensate without it. It's the only thing keeping her even remotely sane."

I stopped all my medication twice. I was hoping once would be enough. The first time, I failed. I lost it. They were right: I went crazy. I was strongly encouraged to take my meds. It was a fight I knew I would not win.

"Patient has been compliant—though hostile." A facade of normalcy regained. High functioning. Working, going to school, socializing. All the things you're supposed to do. All so hollow. The spark was gone. "The medication is effective."

But the drugs felt the same. So, I stopped again. Lots of people do. "Compliance is a major problem in the treatment of mental illness."

I was told that I'd need medication forever. The facts spoke clearly. I was mentally ill. As long as I took my medication, I would be fine. Without it, I was doomed. Why did I want to stop?

I told them how it feels, but it didn't matter. I told them I would recover through force of will alone. "Patient is grandiose."

So, I told them I didn't believe I was sick. "Patient lacks insight."

More Schizophrenics Recover Without Medications than with Them

Percentage of Schizophrenia Patients in Recovery

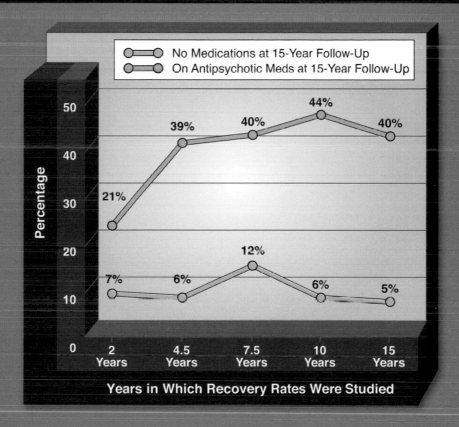

Taken from: Yosim.org, "The Pharmacaust 20,000,000 Dead. So Far." Source: Martin Harrow and Thomas Jobe, "Factors involved in Outcome and Recovery in Schizophrenia Patients Not on Antipsychotic Medications: A 15-year Multifollow-up Study," *Journal of Nervous and Mental Disease*, 195 (2007):406–414.

Many Succeed Without Medication

In truth I was terrified. I believed I was insane, I had failed before, and I wasn't sure I could pull it off on my own. After all, the facts were clear— no one does.

But I did. Later I learned that many have. No one talks about them.

[Mathematician and schizophrenic] John Nash never took medication again—it was key in his recovery. They left that out of the movie [*A Beautiful Mind*].

There are many others who were told no one recovers—told that they would be ill forever—but who proved them wrong.

I am a noncompliant mental patient, yet no one would try to hand me a pill today.

To get here, I had to ignore good medical advice. I had to have poor insight and bad judgment. Without it, I would never have achieved what I have in life.

So, now when I hear about family members who should have made sure their relatives were taking the medication, or courts that should have forced it, I think to myself about doctors who should have listened. I often think about people who may have succeeded in stopping their medication, if only they had the necessary support instead of assurances of failure. I wonder how many more I should be able to name.

I wonder why so few people speak of the validity of the desire to not be medicated. Even a crazy person has a human will.

CHAPTER 3

Personal Narratives

Schizophrenia Alienates a Young Girl from the Real World

Shari Roan

In the following selection Shari Roan describes the devastating impacts of child-onset schizophrenia. Roan tells the story of six-year-old Jani who has frequent bouts of rage and violence, "sees numbers," and lives in a make-believe world populated with rats and cats. It took doctors a while to diagnose Jani's schizophrenia, as the condition is very rare in children. Once she was diagnosed, Jani was prescribed many medications as doctors tried to find something to quell her rage and eliminate her delusional thinking. According to Roan, Jani's parents must constantly struggle to provide stability for Jani, to protect her and others, to get her the help and treatment she needs, and to have hope for her future. Roan writes about health issues for the *Los Angeles Times*.

Photo on previous page. Schizophrenics often fear the real world and have difficulty understanding the effects of their symptoms. (Oscar Burriel/Photo Researchers, Inc.)

I t's been a rough week. A few days ago, at UCLA's [University of California at Los Angeles's] Resnick Neuropsychiatric Hospital, 6-year-old Jani toppled a food cart and was confined to her room. She slammed

SOURCE: Shari Roan, "Jani's at the Mercy of Her Mind," *Los Angeles Times*, June 29, 2009. Copyright © 2009 Los Angeles Times. Reproduced by permission.

her head against the floor, opening a bloody cut that sent her into hysterics. Later, she kicked the hospital therapy dog.

Jani normally likes animals. But most of her animal friends—cats, rats, dogs and birds—are phantoms that only she can see. January Schofield has schizophrenia. Potent psychiatric drugs—in doses that would stagger most adults—seem to skip off her. She is among the rarest of the rare: a child seemingly born mentally ill.

She suffers from delusions, hallucinations and paroxysms of rage so severe that not even her parents feel safe. She's threatened to climb into an oven. She's kicked and tried to bite her little brother. "I'm Jani, and I have a cat named Emily 54," she says, by way of introduction. "And I'm Saturn-the-Rat's baby sitter."

She locks her fingers in front of her chest and flexes her wrists furiously, a tic that surfaces when she's anxious.

She announces that she wants to be a veterinarian. "I'm empathetic with rats," she says. Asked what "empathetic" means, she smiles confidently. "It means you like rats."

The doctors have been trying a new antipsychotic medication, called Moban. Jani knows she is sick and that people want to help her.

"Is the Moban working?" her mother asks Jani during a visit.

"No. I have more friends." Susan Schofield looks crestfallen.

She and her husband, Michael Schofield, have brought French fries. Jani takes a bite, runs around the room and circles back for another bite.

"You want the rats and cats to go away, don't you?" Susan asks, trying to make eye contact with her daughter.

Jani stuffs a French fry into her mouth.

"No," she says. "They're cool. Rats are cool."

Child-Onset Schizophrenia Is Rare

About 1% of adults have schizophrenia: most become ill in their late teens or 20s. Approximately one in 10 will commit suicide.

Doctors and other mental health experts don't fully understand the disease, which has no cure. Jani's extreme early onset has left them almost helpless. The rate of onset in children 13 and under is about one in 30,000 to 50,000. In a national study of 110 children, only one was diagnosed as young as age 6.

"Child-onset schizophrenia is 20 to 30 times more severe than adult-onset schizophrenia," says Dr. Nitin Gogtay, a neurologist at the National Institute of Mental Health who helps direct the children's study, the largest such study in the world on the illness. "Ninety-five percent of the time they are awake these kids are actively hallucinating," Gogtay says. "I don't think I've seen anything more devastating in all of medicine."

For Jani's parents, the most pressing issue is where Jani should live. She has been on the UCLA psych ward—where she was placed during an emergency—since Jan. 16 [2009]. The ward is not designed for long-term care.

Jani can't return to her family's apartment in Valencia. Last fall [2008], she tried to jump out of a second-story window.

Her parents—Michael, a college English instructor, and Susan, a former radio traffic reporter—must decide how to provide as much stability as possible for their daughter while also trying to protect their 18-month-old son.

"If Jani was 16, there would be resources," Michael says. "But very few hospitals, private or public, will take a 6-year-old."

Born Aug. 8, 2002, Jani was different from the start, sleeping fitfully for only about four hours a day. Most infants sleep 14 to 16 hours a day. Only constant, high-energy stimulation kept Jani from screaming.

"For the first 18 months, we would take her to malls, play areas, IKEA [a furniture store], anywhere we could find crowds," says Michael, 33. "It was impossible to overstimulate her. We would leave at 8 in the morning and be gone for 14 hours. We could not come home until Jani had been worn out enough so that she would sleep a couple of hours."

When Jani turned 3, her tantrums escalated. She lasted three weeks in one preschool and one week in another. She demanded to be called by different names; Rainbow one day, Blue-eyed Tree Frog the next. Make-believe friends filled her days—mostly rats and cats and, sometimes, little girls.

She threw her shoes at people when angry and tried to push the car out of gear while Michael was driving. The usual disciplinary strategies parents use to teach their young children proper behavior—time-outs, rules, positive rewards—failed time and again for the Schofields.

"She would go into these rages where she would scream, hit, kick, scratch and bite. She could say, 'Mommy, I love you,' and seconds later switch into being really violent," Michael says.

Kindergarten lasted one week.

A World of Rats

The Schofields consulted doctors and heard myriad opinions: bipolar disorder, attention-deficit hyperactivity disorder, ineffective parenting. No one considered schizophrenia.

In December 2007, they were referred to Dr. Linda Woodall, a psychiatrist in Glendale. Jani's medical re cords for the following year depict a doctor searching for effective medications while her patient slid further into a world stalked by rats and cats.

July 8, 2008: Claps hands, hops (tic-like); food can't touch; strips clothes off if she thinks they have a spot. Wants order and perfection in play, toys, stories.

Nov. 11, 2008: Talking to a "bird named 34" on her hand. Drawing on her clothes and body with permanent marker. Screaming at school and in the waiting room.

Jan. 7, 2009: Patient is psychotic; talking to rats naming them the days of the week. . . . I believe it would be in the best interests of January and her family to have her placed in residential treatment.

Her parents named her January because they loved the sound of it. But this year, the month of January became the breaking point for a fragile family. Jani's torment had escalated through much of 2008. She was hospitalized last fall for three weeks.

Jani tried, and failed, again to attend school. She choked herself with her hands, hit her head on the walls and said she wanted to die. "Home was a nightmare, and school was a nightmare," Michael says.

A new imaginary friend named 400-the-Cat moved in. He told her to kick and hit other people. "We realized she didn't control her imaginary friends. They controlled her," Michael says. Many phantoms populated her mind now: two little girls named 100 Degrees and 24 Hours; 200-the-Rat; Magical 61-the-Cat; and 400.

Susan, 39, was laid off from her job in September, and although money was tight, she felt almost relieved. Jani needed constant supervision.

Woodall decided to try a new drug, Haldol, 1 milligram, twice a day. It seemed to calm Jani, and 400-the-Cat went away.

The Schofields made another attempt at first grade, sending Jani to school Jan. 12. But that day, the muscles on the left side of her body locked up, and the school called paramedics. She had developed dystonia, a movement disorder that causes involuntary contractions of muscles. It's a side effect of high doses of some psychotropic medications.

FAST FACT

According to Mental Health America, adult schizophrenia is sixty times more common than childhood schizophrenia.

On Jan. 16, Michael dropped his daughter off at school again. "She seemed fine that morning," he said. She was taking a lower dose of Haldol plus medications to quell psychosis and stabilize mood.

But at 9:15, she began screaming that she wanted to see her brother, Bodhi. She threw her pencils and shoes, tried to jump out of the classroom window, then ran down the halls. The assistant principal called Michael and told him to come and take his daughter home.

Michael was drained. "I knew if we took her home we couldn't get any help anywhere," he says. "We were fed up with nobody believing us, nobody helping us."

He refused.

The principal called the Los Angeles County Sheriff's Department and reported that the parents had abandoned their misbehaving child. Three school psychologists were summoned by the assistant principal, and a sheriff's deputy called for a team of emergency psychiatric workers.

Jani was locked in an empty office playing with 24 Hours. The experts concluded she was psychotic and took her to UCLA.

Little Hope for Recovery

Each day, before the Schofields visit, they stop at a Burger King for lunch and order take-out for Jani. "So many people just thought we had a bratty kid," says Michael, feeding Bodhi as he squirms in a high chair in the restaurant. "UCLA was the first to tell us: 'It's not your fault—there is something wrong with her brain.'"

When her family arrives, Jani looks surprised to see them although they visit every day. She is wearing a lime-green T-shirt and pink skirt with turquoise rubber shoes. Her hair is tousled. Her legs carry the last traces of baby fat. Susan dabs toothpaste on a toothbrush and runs it over her daughter's teeth for a few seconds—the only dental care Jani will allow.

"I'd rather be 16," Jani says, putting a hand on her hip and tossing a flirty look over her shoulder. "I'm 14 on weekends, Thursdays, Wednesdays and Tuesdays."

She pauses. "All except for Mondays."

She loves Littlest Pet Shop toys, miniature animals with houses and furniture, and stacks them on a shelf in her room.

Although she can't sit still long enough to read a book, she is a voracious learner. She's also bright—her IQ is 146. Over the years, Michael and Susan have entertained her by feeding her information well beyond her years: specifics of evolution, the Roman Empire, the periodic table of elements.

"What is the atomic symbol for tungsten?" Susan asks.

"W."

Jani talks about living in Calalini. Where is Calalini? She leans in to whisper her secret. "Calalini is on the border between this world and my other world."

Jani's psychiatrist at UCLA, Dr. Karen Lim, has tried several medications. A whopping 300 milligrams of Thorazine manages to stop the psychosis, but it too causes dystonia.

Michael worries that the heavy doses of medication might kill his daughter. But without it, she might kill herself. Jani had recently told Michael that the temperature in Calalini had risen to 200 degrees—a sign that her hallucinations are worsening. She also says that 400-the-Cat is being really bossy.

On a mid-April afternoon, Michael and Susan meet with Lim and Jani's social worker, Georgia Wagniere, to discuss the rejections from two residential facilities that primarily care for children who have been abused or neglected but are not severely mentally ill. No one wants to take in a 6-year-old schizophrenic.

"I feel like we're back to zero again," Michael says.

Susan proposes that the couple trade in their two-bedroom apartment and rent two one-bedroom units in the same complex. One parent would live with Bodhi and one with Jani on alternating days.

The group discusses the stress on the couple. Both Michael and Susan have relatives who were mentally ill, and both struggle with depression and take antidepressants. They receive no help from their families.

"It's been very taxing," Wagniere says. "It has disrupted your entire life; your finances, your mental status."

"I'm prepared to go the rest of my life like this," Michael says. "I'm not hanging on to the hope that she'll get better. My biggest fear is that she won't live to 18."

"I have more hope," Susan says softly, staring at the floor.

Bodhi begins fussing. Michael and Susan thank Wagniere and Lim and leave to visit Jani.

Lim gathers her papers and follows them down the hall. She has recently issued a formal diagnosis of child-onset schizophrenia. The case has tested the limits of the young doctor's expertise. "Jani knows she is different from other children," she says. "She has a degree of insight. She says, 'If my parents don't love me, I'll go live with my rats.'"

Lim sighs. "I would like to give the parents more hope that she won't kill herself."

She catches up to Michael and Susan and unlocks the three heavy security doors that separate the children's unit from the rest of the hospital. Jani's hair is pulled back in a braid. She begins to show off her Littlest Pet Shops.

A boy hospitalized on the unit passes by the open door of Jani's room and slams it shut. A stunned look crosses Jani's face. She pauses for a few seconds, then marches across the room announcing she is going to hit the boy. Michael stops her and tries to redirect her attention to her Pet Shop. But she turns on him, jumping and butting her head under his chin.

He winces and holds her arms as she kicks him in the legs, butts her head into his chest and tries to bite him through his T-shirt. "I just want to hit him! I just want to hit him!"

Hospital staff rush in and restrain her on the bed. Jani's wailing rings down the hall. "I just want to hit him!"

About 20 minutes later, a tired Michael emerges from the room to drive home with Susan and Bodhi. "She's calm now," he says. "But the next time she sees him, she'll hit him."

Some Positive Steps

Finally, a break. A combination of Tegretol, Thorazine and lithium has blunted some of the rage and coaxed a few of the phantoms from Jani's mind. Lim discharges her June 1 after 133 days in the hospital.

The two apartments are ready. Jani will live in 925; Bodhi, just across the parking lot in 1035. Jani's apartment is modeled after the psychiatric ward. Her room has only a bed so that, during a tantrum, she can be placed where she won't hurt herself. The living room is called the day room and is packed with toys and games. The kitchen is the supply room.

The Schofields bought walkie-talkies to communicate between apartments. Michael has written Jani's schedule on a large white board, just like the hospital staff did: 14:00, occupational therapy; 15:00, quiet time; 16:00, outdoors; 17:00, dinner; 18:00, recreational therapy. Whoever stays with Jani at night is referred to as her "staff."

Michael has been worried about paying rent on two places. But, he says, "We want her home. When she's not in Calalini—where they all are—we can have a relationship with her. We want to take what we can get."

The Schofields have sought home-based special services but aren't hopeful. They've tried to get respite care from a center that helps people with developmental disabilities but were told the service was available only for parents of autistic children.

"We've developed sort of a bunker mentality," Michael says. "Every time Susan and I have relied on other people, we've been disappointed."

Jani's school, however, will take her back, in a special-education classroom.

The family arrives at Jani's new home around 3 p.m. on a Monday. "Honey!" Jani shouts, running across the parking lot to hug the family dog she hasn't seen in 4 1/2 months.

The wide-eyed, penetrating gaze Jani wore in the hospital—when she stared as if trying to see into a person's brain—is gone. She has spoken little of 400-the-Cat in recent days. But she flaps her hands and rarely stops moving as Michael and Susan show her a cupboard full of prizes she can earn with good behavior. As she becomes familiar with the three small rooms, she begins to relax. She laughs when Bodhi fusses. Friends have come by to visit and share in the homecoming.

"This is actually a very happy day," says Michael, as he takes in the scene. "She has beaten back probably the most severe mental illness known to man. My hope now is that we can maintain this stability for a while."

Jani opens the door to a small balcony where her parents have set up an easel with paper, markers, paints and chalk. She grabs chalk, scribbles on the board and looks up at her parents, grinning.

"Oh-oh," says Susan, with a sigh. She steps back and calls for Michael to have a look. He does. He says nothing.

400.

Schizophrenia Stole My Son

Kathy Harkey

In the following essay, Kathy Harkey writes about her son and how he lost his battle with mental illness. According to Harkey, her son did not understand he was sick. Under state law he could not be forced to take medications or receive other treatment for his mental illness unless he was considered dangerous. Harkey agonizes over the fact that until the night he took his own life, her son never qualified for the treatment he so desperately needed. Harkey advocates for changes to the mental health system in America. Her essay appeared in the newsletter for the Treatment Advocacy Center, a nonprofit organization dedicated to eliminating barriers to treatment for the mentally ill.

Two years ago, on an early winter morning, I searched the horse pastures and woods around my country home to locate my son Joshua. Out of character, Joshua had not come home the night before. I worried about him. You see, Joshua suffered from a mental illness.

SOURCE: Kathy Harkey, "For the Love of Joshua," *Catalyst*, Winter 2008–2009, pp. 1, 5. Copyright © 2008–2009 Treatment Advocacy Center. Reproduced by permission.

He Could Not Get the Treatment He Needed

Before Joshua could receive the care he needed, Virginia law required that his brain disorder become so unbearable and painful that he act dangerously. Joshua was very sick, but like many people with a mental illness, he did not understand he was sick. Trapped by laws, my prayers turned away from seeing my son achieve his dreams of becoming an electrical engineer and raising a family. Instead, I prayed he would act irrationally without getting hurt so I could finally get him the help he needed.

Because of Virginia State law—which requires that a mental patient act dangerously in order to receive treatment—Joshua Harkey was unable seek the treatment he so urgently needed for his schizophrenia. (© Andre Jenny/Alamy)

Joshua's condition was treatable, but he never became dangerous. Virginia law did not put significance on Joshua's pain and his obvious need for treatment. As time passed, the illness, symptoms, and torment grew worse. Joshua suffered in quiet agony.

Late one night, Joshua's mental anguish reached a point that even he, a strong young man of 24 years, could not bear. I was in bed reading beside my husband Barry when I heard Joshua release a wail of agony so deep it sent shivers down my spine. I jumped out of bed running toward Joshua's room. Barry ran alongside, dialing 911 on a cordless phone. Within minutes, medical personnel arrived. Standing by my side, they sympathetically looked at Joshua.

The wounded, unfocused expression in Joshua's eyes stabbed my heart. He stood stiffly against his bedroom wall unable to move, catatonic, making whimpering noises of despair. Tears pooling in my eyes, I sent a pleading look for aid to the rescue workers. They looked back in helplessness and pity. They wanted to help Joshua, but could not. He did not meet Virginia's criteria. By state standards, Joshua still was not considered dangerous to anyone. It did not matter that Joshua was hurting unbearably with a treatable condition. It did not matter that he was covered by my excellent health insurance. State law blocked the medical care my son desperately needed.

On that chilly morning of January 8, 2006, after hours of relentless searching, Joshua was spotted a few feet inside the woods. He lay in the small fort he had built with his two younger brothers when he was nine years old. Sitting beside him was an old rusted Tonka truck he'd received for Christmas years earlier.

The Illness Finally Brought Him to His Knees

The illness had finally brought Joshua to his knees. He had reached the stage where he could endure no more.

Joshua was lifeless. Alone in the woods near the home where he grew up, Joshua died by his own hand. His head now lay—not soft in sleep—but tilted at an odd angle against the base of the tree that supported the well-weathered fort. Joshua finally met Virginia's criteria for receiving medical care—but it was too late, all hope was lost.

State laws prevented treatment, allowed the painful progression of schizophrenia, and forced me to stand by and helplessly watch Joshua's illness take the ultimate toll. I am now forced to live each day knowing Joshua is gone forever.

> **FAST FACT**
>
> Suicide is the leading cause of premature death in people diagnosed with schizophrenia.

I now have a new mission in life. I advocate for changes in America's failing mental health system—changes that will prevent needless suffering and deaths like that of my son. I could not save my own beloved son, but I fight to spare other mothers and fathers from this agonizing experience. I work to fix a broken system so that people with mental illnesses can receive the timely treatment they need. I advocate because I know that Joshua, with his kind, warm heart, would want me to do all I can to open doors for people like him to gain access to medical care.

I cannot bring my son back, but I can pray—prayers are eternal. To everyone reading my story, please pray for Joshua, my family, and all of the policymakers whose eyes need to be opened so that positive change can be made to America's failing mental health system before more precious lives are lost.

Growing Up with a Schizophrenic Mother

Susan Nathiel

In the following excerpt from Susan Nathiel's book *Daughters of Madness*, two adult women describe their middle-childhood memories of life at home with their schizophrenic mothers. According to Nathiel, middle childhood—generally six to eleven years old—is what we think of when we remember being a child. It is also a very important time in childhood development. The women describe mothers who barely took care of themselves, let alone their children, and who were often angry, depressed, unpredictable, and paranoid. Nathiel is a psychotherapist, author, and founding member of the Center for Illness in Families.

When we think of being a kid, middle childhood is usually the time we're remembering. We're old enough to have "explicit" memories—such memories start at about age three—and by that time we have a store of memories of events and of specific things that happened to us. When we remember them, we have the feeling of "I'm remembering this happening," which is quite different from the feeling of the implicit memories we have from birth to about age three. If things are going pretty well, our memories may be episodic (more like snapshots than videos) but come fully equipped with sights, sounds, feelings and sensations, tastes, and smells.

Kids this age have a daunting number of developmental tasks as their brains keep growing. They learn how to think logically during this time, and about how others think and feel. They build on their ability to relate to other people, connect with them, play, work together, and form friendships. A core sense of social identity begins during this period, to be modified during adolescence. Kids are learning about morality but haven't yet moved from black-and-white, right-and-wrong thinking. At five or six they begin going to school, inhabiting for the first time a world of their own outside the family and home. They relate on their own to new adults and other children, and their intellectual and cognitive abilities begin to take center stage.

A Young Child's Understanding of the World

Ideally, kids this age can explore the world on their own, while also knowing there's a safe place to go home to, literally and figuratively. The best case is when parents can, from a distance, support their children's move out into the world, being ready to back them up, provide comfort and support, and encourage them to keep going. Children this age also need to be protected from being taken advantage of, whether by adults or other kids, and they need to know that their parents are paying enough attention to notice when things aren't right, to ask questions, to sense significant changes. This doesn't mean shadowing kids and protecting them from everything, no matter how small; there's a broad range of okay parenting between the extremes of neglect, on the one hand, and the worst stereotype of yuppie overparenting, on the other.

When kids from dysfunctional families are old enough to start seeing the inside of other people's families, it's usually something they don't forget. This may be the first time they've ever seen a more "normal" family in action, and it may be the first realization that what goes on in their family is not the way it is for everyone. This age is often the beginning of a decades-long search for answers to the question, "Why did things happen the way they did in my family?" Ask anyone who grew up in a very dysfunctional family how they felt about things when they were four or five, and you'll just get a blank look, even if family life was violent, crazy, or bizarre. "It's just the way it was. I didn't feel anything in particular" is the usual answer. No, they don't feel any particular way "about" it because that usually comes later, when they're old enough to reflect on their experience and when they've seen other possibilities. Kids who lose a parent to death, divorce, or abandonment very early on don't usually have a sense of missing that parent—life without them is just the way it is. Later on, they can reflect on what they missed, how things might have been different, but at the time, the way daily life unfolds in the family is the way reality is taken in by the young child.

First let's look at daily life in families with mentally ill mothers. For almost all the women interviewed their mothers were symptomatic during this period, if not before. . . .

When we get a look at what happened behind closed doors in these families, the differences among various kinds of mental illness become relevant. . . .

June's Mother

The mothers with schizophrenia or other unclear psychotic illnesses could be unpredictable and often bizarre in their behavior, or seem remote and unreachable. June's mother was clearly struggling with dissociation when June was young, but became more overtly disturbed and impaired after her first hospitalization, when June was ten. It was around this time that she was given two diagnoses: schizophrenia and multiple personality disorder. Her relationship with her daughters deteriorated over the course of several years.

June: *Before I was ten, she was better. She would be at the bus stop when I came home from school, and she would make my lunch to take to school. I remember feeling like I could rely on her for those things. She would ask me what happened at school, that kind of thing. And she might play with me, put shaving cream on the table and draw pictures in it, stuff like that. That was fun. Holidays were okay; she would decorate the house. Those were the better memories.*

Even during those years, there would be a lot of times she just checked out. She would be sitting there looking at her nails and she'd just be gone. She'd just act like you weren't even there. The thing with the nails didn't change when she got sicker. No matter what, her nails were always manicured and beautiful, and they were her thing. But she got hospitalized when I was ten, I don't remember exactly how it happened, and then I just stopped trusting her, she got so unpredictable and crazy. She got much more angry after that. And she just basically stopped functioning as our mother. We would be dirty and smelly and wouldn't bathe for days on end, but her nails were always done. She would sit at the table and look at her nails and smoke cigarettes.

Once I told her I wanted to take a bath, and she asked me why, like it never occurred to her anybody should take a bath. When she was better, before that first hospitalization, she would go to the store with us, and afterwards she wouldn't. She had always been afraid they would lock her up, and they finally did. She got so much worse after that. And she would ask me to stay home from school and keep her company a lot. Sometimes I did. I had to kind of figure out for myself what I should do. Before she went to the hospital that first time, she would just go to bed if she was

> **FAST FACT**
>
> According to studies, as many as 50 percent of women with schizophrenia become mothers, but about one-third of women with schizophrenia lose custody of their children.

depressed. Afterwards she was just so dissociated so much of the time.

She just wasn't there. That's what I realize now. She wasn't anxious or upset, just not there. Then she would just change, and I couldn't figure out what was going on. Sometimes I would come home and she would say, "Who are you? Get out of my house," and she'd threaten to call the cops. She had no idea who I was. I was always afraid she was going to call the police, and they would come and see that she's insane, and they would take me away from my sister.

After she was in the hospital the first time, she would just sleep in the morning and stopped getting us up in the morning, and we had to do that for ourselves. My older sister started being away from the house a lot more, and me and my other sister were on our own. My hair was long and tangled, and I would just shove it in some kind of big clip.

A friend of mine at school kept saying to wear my hair down, and I would always say, "Oh, I forgot this morning," but it was just a rat's nest, and finally my sister had to chop it off.

When we came home after school there was no structure at all. There wasn't any dinnertime or any rules about homework, or whatever. My dinner would be Cap'n Crunch cereal out of the box while I watched TV. Sometimes I would do homework, and sometimes I wouldn't. I just did whatever I wanted. Once my oldest sister was on the front stoop drinking wine out of a bottle, and my mother got mad at her, not because of what she was doing but because the neighbors might object to it.

Tess's Mother

Tess's mother was periodically overtly psychotic and paranoid, acting very strangely in public. She did seem to try to follow some household structure, but was barely able to do that. . . .

Tess: *She would get us up in the morning and get us off to school. Looking back, that was amazing that she could even do it. We had uniforms, so that made things easier. And she would do the dishes, but she couldn't do a lot of the other household chores. She cried a lot, and you could also hear her whispering to herself. But she absolutely could not take care of herself. She wouldn't bathe, she wouldn't change her own clothes, she'd have the same clothes on for days and days. She was always disheveled, her face was always dirty. I remember dust balls hanging from her hair. That's how I remember my mother.*

We couldn't go to the relatives for the holidays, or if we did we'd have to rush, because we always knew Mommy was home alone, crying and sad. So, how could you be happy to be out of the house? She wouldn't come, no matter what anybody said, and then sometimes we just had to stay home. Nobody could ever come to our house, because she didn't trust anyone at all.

When we were at school, the only thing she did was listen to Italian radio—no TV. She didn't trust anybody, so she didn't have any friends, never went out by herself. My father could sometimes persuade her to go out with us to the supermarket on a Friday night. He'd have to beg, though: "Maria, Maria, let's all go out, please. People aren't looking at you. Come on." Sometimes she'd pick up the phone and just start screaming at whoever had called. And then she'd hang up, and she'd just be crying and crying and crying. If one of us kids were there, we'd be trying to talk her out of it, talk her down. Then, and I don't know where this came from, she'd go through periods where she was just obsessive about stuff—washing her hands all the time, checking the lights and the stove, checking over and over again to make sure things were turned off. And checking the door to make sure it was locked. Open, close, lock, unlock, open, close, lock—that would go on forever. And those are memories of my mother, growing up.

My Brother Is Schizophrenic and Homeless

Glenn Grunwald

In the following editorial, Canadian businessman Glen Grunwald talks about the plight of his schizophrenic brother and what public policies might be enacted to help him and other homeless and mentally ill people in Canada and the United States. According to Grunwald, his brother has been struggling with schizophrenia for almost thirty years. He has been homeless, been in and out of jail, and tried to kill himself. Grunwald believes government policies that address homelessness and mental illness must be linked together in order to help his brother and others like him. Grunwald is vice president for basketball operations of the New York Knicks and former general manager of the Toronto Raptors.

The calls come at all hours of the day and night. Most often collect, but not always. Sometimes there's a prim, somewhat disapproving, message which lets me know the call is collect and coming from a jail. I never know what to expect when I pick up the

SOURCE: Glen Grunwald, "My Brother, the Homeless Person," *Toronto Star,* March 11, 2005, p. A21. Copyright © 2005 Toronto Star Newspapers, Ltd. Reproduced by permission of the author.

phone. The calm voice of a middle-aged man? His alter ego, the conspiracy theorist? Or the alcoholic who will say anything for a chance to calm his demons?

My brother, my only sibling, is homeless and schizophrenic in America. His 25-plus years on the road has given me a unique perspective on the homeless debate here in Toronto. Like *Toronto Star* columnist Jocy Slinger, who has frequently written on the homeless, I have sadly concluded that homelessness and mental illness are inextricably linked.

A Vicious Disease

In my brother's case, the viciousness of the disease and the capriciousness it provokes, makes it almost impossible to help him. An example: I once flew to Seattle to get his signature on papers so he could have his own bank card and I could then send him money without the hassles of a Western Union wire transfer. He refused because he saw a conspiracy behind my motives. Gary was diagnosed as a paranoid schizophrenic in 1978. He was only 20, poised on the brink of manhood, and a lifelong love of aviation had just culminated in his certification as an aircraft mechanic. With his illness, the job he had landed at O'Hare airport in Chicago evaporated, along with the rest of his life.

The skies guide Gary today, causing him to beat an odd flight path between Tucson, Arizona—where his fascination of airplanes leads him to the boneyards of mothballed planes—and Seattle, Washington, which is home to Boeing Field and the national Museum of Flight.

It was in Tucson two years ago, in the summer of 2003, that Gary almost died, not once, but twice. He had been in jail there, incarcerated on one of the dozens of petty charges he's faced over the years. The prison had released him in the early hours of morning, simply shoving him out the door with no food, no clothes and nowhere to go.

As usual, we got the call. And, as usual, I had the same impossible dilemma my family faced over the years: Did I send him money so he could have a roof over his head and food to eat, and then wait for the inevitable crisis to put him back in hospital or jail? Or try to force him to get the health care he so desperately needs—but does not want—by forcing him into an impotent and seemingly non-existent mental health-care system in Arizona?

In this case, I told him to find a motel. I never send him money directly anymore (beyond what he needs immediately to eat) because he ends up drinking it away or, worse, being beaten and robbed.

Gary called back a while later to say he'd found a small motel in the Howard Johnson chain where the staff didn't seem to be alarmed by his appearance or demeanour. I talked to the desk, then sent them my credit card number.

My brother distinguished himself within an hour by robbing the tip jar from the front counter. But instead of calling the police, these people called us. It was the start of a summer-long relationship.

The room came with a free breakfast in the morning. One of the women rummaged through the lost-and-found to pull out clothing to fit his emaciated 6-foot, 4-inch frame. Another one would invite him to share her pizza on the night shift. And she would always make an extra hot chocolate before bedtime.

It was a heart-warming story but I long ago learned there are no happy endings.

No Happy Endings

Gary seemed to have the run of the place and the support of its staff but he had no steady medication and no professional overseeing his mental health. He began to have breakdowns, hallucinations that would scare other guests. He would phone, making wild claims about how my wife had murdered his (non-existent) family. When he got like this, the motel staff would call 911, the hospital would hold him for a day or two, medicate him, release him and then the cycle would start again.

Worst of all, as the summer wore on, he began to talk about killing himself. We returned from the wedding of Raptor basketball player Alvin Williams in Philadelphia to find my brother had been hospitalized for what the psychiatric staff deemed to be an "accidental" overdose.

The diagnosis stuck despite my protestations that he had been talking about suicide and they released him.

The real crisis came a week later. Gary called our house to say he was going to kill himself with a knife.

While I spoke to him, my wife called the front desk on her cell phone. The woman called back a minute or so later. "It's bad news," she said. "There's blood everywhere and I don't know where he is."

> ## FAST FACT
>
> According to the Substance Abuse and Mental Health Services Administration, 20 to 25 percent of the homeless population in the United States suffers from some form of severe mental illness.

When the paramedics arrived, they found him in the bushes where he'd crawled off to die. "I don't know how anybody survived this," said the man on the phone. "The room is totalled. There's blood everywhere."

But Gary did survive. We called the motel the next day to take responsibility for the damages.

"Don't worry about it," said the manager soothingly. "It's just blood. We can clean it up."

When thanked for all the care they had shown Gary, he brushed it aside. "It sounds kinda weird but, you know, it's like he's one of the family."

My wife hung up. And wept at the unexpected kindness of strangers.

However well-intentioned, it was a kindness that was killing Gary. They gave him, literally, just enough rope to hang himself. It is a situation which I believe is played out time and again on the streets of Toronto.

I see Gary in every makeshift bed and inhabited grate. I see him in the hollow eyes of those who hold their hands out for help. I see him in the screeching alcoholics who frighten passersby. I understand why people shy away. It is easier to dehumanize than to deal with the difficult person inside. . . .

I recognize the complexity of the issue of homelessness and the need for a multi-pronged solution. It affects all of us in Toronto as a moral issue and is a direct reflection of our quality of life.

One component of the solution is the creation of affordable housing supported by all levels of government. . . .

Homelessness and Mental Illness Are Linked

The private sector is willing to be part of the solution but, in return, public policy must make it easier and simpler to acquire land and financing. On a personal note, I believe there must be further formal linkage between homelessness and mental illness.

No amount of nudging would help my brother; he needed an outright shove. Frightened by his near-death experience, he agreed to return to Seattle where he is a familiar face to many of the mental health workers there. It hasn't been easy. Once there, tough love soon devolved to no love and he wound up in jail for a lengthy stretch. He finally ended up before a judge who simply shortened his leash. Gary is on probation. He has a caring social worker who has scrupulously managed his Social Security Disability benefits while he was away. My brother is often too sick to even pick up his own money.

So now, he has his own room in a supervised hotel, and money doled out to him from a small but steady source of income.

He reports to his parole officer every day. If he drinks, he's back in jail. If he takes drugs, he goes back. If he doesn't take his medications, there too, are consequences.

Glenn Grunwald's experiences with his homeless and schizophrenic brother have made him an advocate for government policies that link mental illness and homelessness. **(Ron Turenne/NBAE via Getty Images)**

Another dilemma. An example of the criminalization of mental illness? Yes.

The only way my brother will participate in the medical programs he so desperately needs without being institutionalized or jailed? Yes.

An alternative to his homelessness? Yes.

Should there be a better way? Yes.

Until then, I want my brother to be a criminal rather than another suicide. I want my brother to be in a supervised rooming house instead of living on the street.

Part of my brother's new probation package has been his own telephone calling card and he uses it frequently, just to check in. He's calmer and, although I can't honestly say he's happy, there are days you can say he's content.

And he has moments of clarity that are wrenching.

My brother called one night and asked how I was doing. "I've got a cold," I said somewhat peevishly.

"I haven't had one in a long time," he replied.

"Well, you're not missing much."

There was a beat before he spoke.

"Oh," he said. "I miss plenty."

It breaks my heart to think on it. But I know it to be true.

GLOSSARY

acute schizophrenia A disorder in which the symptoms of schizophrenia occur abruptly; they may subside or become chronic.

affect The expression of emotion displayed to others through facial expressions, hand gestures, tone of voice. Types of affect include: flat (inanimate, no expression); blunted (minimally responsive); inappropriate (incongruous expressions of emotion relative to the content of a conversation); and labile (sudden and abrupt changes in type and intensity of emotion).

akathisia A syndrome characterized by unpleasant sensations of "inner" restlessness that manifests itself with an inability to sit still or remain motionless. A side effect of antipsychotic medications.

anhedonia Loss of the capacity to experience pleasure. A symptom of schizophrenia and major depression.

anosognosia Lack of awareness of the nature of one's illness.

atypical antipsychotics A group of medications used for the treatment of psychotic symptoms in schizophrenia and other psychiatric disorders. Atypical antipsychotics were introduced for the treatment of schizophrenia in the 1990s and can be differentiated from earlier "typical antipsychotics" in their mode of action. Atypical antipsychotics generally act on the neurotransmitter serotonin. Atypical antipsychotics include Abilify and clozapine.

auditory hallucination A symptom in a schizophrenic or psychotic mood disorder that, in the absence of an external source, consists of hearing a voice or other auditory stimulus that other people do not perceive.

catatonia Disturbance of motor behavior with either extreme stupor or random, purposeless activity.

delusion A false belief that is resistant to reason or contrary to actual fact. Common delusions in schizophrenia include delusions of persecution, delusions about one's importance (sometimes called delusions of grandeur), or delusions of being controlled by others.

dementia praecox　A late–nineteenth-century term for schizophrenia.

dopamine　A neurotransmitter that acts within certain brain cells to help regulate emotions and movement. Some of the symptoms of schizophrenia are related to excessive levels of dopamine activity in a part of the brain called the striatum.

dystonia　Painful, involuntary muscle cramps or spasms; one of the side effects associated with antipsychotic medications.

first-rank symptoms　A list of symptoms considered to be diagnostic of schizophrenia. These include delusions, somatic hallucinations, hearing voices commenting on one's behavior, and thought insertion or withdrawal. First-rank symptoms are sometimes called Schneiderian symptoms.

hallucination　A false sensory perception. A person experiencing a hallucination may hear sounds or see people or objects that are not present. Hallucinations can also affect the senses of smell, touch, and taste.

hebephrenic schizophrenia　A severe disintegration of personality. An older term for what was later known as the disorganized subtype of schizophrenia.

Huntington's chorea　A hereditary disease that typically appears in midlife, marked by gradual loss of brain function and voluntary movement. Some of its symptoms resemble those of schizophrenia.

kalirin　A protein implicated in causing schizophrenia, named for the multiple-handed Hindu goddess Kali for its ability to interact with numerous other proteins.

morbidity　The unhealthiness or disease characteristics associated with a mental disorder.

negative symptoms　Symptoms of schizophrenia that represent a loss or reduction of normal functioning.

neuroleptic　Another name for the older type of antipsychotic medications— typical antipsychotics—given to schizophrenic patients.

paranoia   A severe but relatively rare mental disorder characterized by the presence of systematized delusions, often of a persecutory character, involving being followed, poisoned, or harmed by other means, in an otherwise intact personality.

parkinsonism   A set of symptoms originally associated with Parkinson's disease that can occur as side effects of neuroleptic medications. The symptoms include trembling of the fingers or hands, a shuffling gait, and tight or rigid muscles.

polygenic   A trait or disorder that is determined by a group of genes acting together. Most human characteristics, including height, weight, and general body build, are polygenic. Schizophrenia and late-onset Alzheimer's disease are considered polygenic disorders.

positive symptoms   Symptoms of schizophrenia that represent excesses or distortions of normal mental functions.

prognosis   A forecast of the probable course and/or outcome of a disease.

psychosis   A severe state that is characterized by loss of contact with reality and deterioration in normal social functioning; examples are schizophrenia and paranoia. Psychosis is usually one feature of an overarching disorder, not a disorder in itself.

referential   A type of delusion in which the person misinterprets items, minor occurrences, or other people's behavior as referring to him- or herself.

schizophrenia   A chronic mental disease marked by disturbances in thinking, emotional responsiveness, and behavior. The disease comes from the Greek roots *schizo* ("split") and *phrene* ("mind") to describe the fragmented thinking of people with the disorder.

Schneiderian symptoms   Another name for first-rank symptoms of schizophrenia, named after Kurt Schneider, the German psychiatrist who listed them in 1959.

serotonin   A neurotransmitter that may have a role in schizophrenia. Serotonin regulates various functions, including mood, appetite, sleep, muscle contraction, and some cognitive functions, including memory and learning.

striatum	A part of the basal ganglia, a deep structure in the cerebrum of the brain. Abnormally high levels of dopamine in the striatum are thought to be related to the delusions and hallucinations of schizophrenia.
tactile hallucination	A false perception of movement or sensation, as from an amputated limb, or a crawling sensation on the skin.
tardive dyskinesia	A condition that involves involuntary movements of the tongue, jaw, mouth, face, or other groups of skeletal muscles that usually occurs either late in antipsychotic therapy or after the therapy is discontinued. It may be irreversible.
typical antipsychotics	The first generation of antipsychotic medications. These medications are also called neuroleptics or major tranquilizers. Typical antipsychotics work differently from newer "atypical antipsychotics." Typical antipsychotics include thorazine and haloperidol.
Wilson's disease	A rare hereditary disease marked by high levels of copper deposits in the brain and liver. It can cause psychiatric symptoms resembling schizophrenia.

CHRONOLOGY

B.C.   **ca. 2000**   The "Book of Hearts" within an ancient Egyptian medical treatise called the Ebers papyrus contains descriptions of the symptoms of mental conditions including schizophrenia.

     ca. 400   The Greek physician Hippocrates states that the brain is the seat of intelligence and is involved in sensation.

A.D. ca. 400–500   Mental disorders in the Middle Ages are seen as evil spirits that possess the body.

     ca. 900   The book *Leechdom, Wortcunning and Star Craft* of early England gives herbal remedies for hallucinations, mental vacancy, dementia, and folly.

     ca. 1020   Persian physician Avicenna's *The Canon of Medicine* describes a condition resembling schizophrenia, which it refers to as *junun mufrit* (severe madness), clearly distinguished from other forms of madness such as mania, rabies, and manic depressive psychosis.

     1564   Giulio Cesare Aranzi (aka Julius Caesar Arantius) names a region of the brain "the hippocampus."

     1755   J.B. Le Roy uses electroconvulsive therapy for mental illness.

     1797   A detailed case report about James Tilly Matthews is written and is considered to be the first fully documented case of paranoid schizophrenia.

     1812   Benjamin Rush writes the first American book on psychiatry, *Medical Inquiries and Observations upon the Diseases of the Mind.*

1870s	Karl Ludwig Kahlbaum describes and names catatonia. Along with Ewald Hecker, Kahlbaum also develops the concept of hebephrenia.
1880	Seven categories of mental illness are used for U.S. census data: mania, melancholia, monomania, paresis, dementia, dipsomania, and epilepsy.
ca. 1887	German psychiatrist Emil Kraepelin identifies schizophrenia (he calls it dementia praecox) as a distinct mental disorder. Kraepelin is the first to make a distinction between schizophrenia and manic depression.
1891	Wilhelm von Waldeyer coins the term *neuron*.
1897	Charles Scott Sherrington coins the term *synapse*.
1903	The British neurologist, Thomas R. Elliott proposes the concept of chemical neurotransmitters.
1909	Clifford Beers founds the organization currently named Mental Health America.
1911	Eugen Bleuler coins the term *schizophrenia* and describes its symptoms as either positive or negative.
1930s	Schizophrenia is treated by inducing convulsions, first with an injection of camphor and later with electroconvulsive therapy.
1949	Australian psychiatrist John Cade introduces the use of lithium to treat psychosis.
1952	Henri Laborit discovers the drug chlorpromazine (Thorazine), the first of the typical antipsychotics used to treat psychosis.
1952	The first edition of the the *Diagnostic and Statistical Manual of Mental Disorders* (*DSM*) is published by the American Psychiatric Association.

1953   Betty Twarog and Irvine Page identify serotonin in the brain.

1954   Chlorpromazine (Thorazine) is approved by the U.S. Food and Drug Administration for the treatment of psychosis.

1956   Gregory Bateson, Don Jackson, Jay Haley, and John Weakland publish *Toward a Theory of Schizophrenia.*

1959   Kurt Schneider divides the symptoms of schizophrenia into primary, or "first-rank" symptoms, and secondary, or "second-rank" symptoms.

1960s   A large number of schizophrenics and other seriously mentally ill people are moved out of large state institutions, or "deinstitutionalized." The state hospitals are closed down.

1961   Thomas Szasz publishes *The Myth of Mental Illness*, in which he argues that psychiatric disorders, including schizophrenia, do not exist.

1963   The U.S. Community Mental Health Act is passed, which provides for the development of a network of community-based mental health services. It contributes to "deinstitutionalization."

1971   Clozapine, the first atypical antipsychotic medication, is used to treat schizophrenia in Europe.

1975   Clozapine is removed from the market due to concerns over side effects.

1976   The first study of schizophrenia using computed tomography (CT) is published.

1984   The first magnetic resonance imaging study of schizophrenia is published.

1986   The National Alliance for Research on Schizophrenia and Depression is formed.

1989   The U.S. Food and Drug Administration approves clozapine, but only for treatment-resistant schizophrenia.

1990s   The atypical antipsychotics—olanzapine, risperidon, and quetiapine—are introduced and gain widespread use because they do not cause as many side effects as the typical antipsychotics.

2000   The *DSM* IV-TR is published. It contains five subclassifications of schizophrenia: paranoid type; disorganized type; catatonic type; undifferentiated type; and residual type.

1999–2012   Discussions are conducted on the diagnostic criteria for schizophrenia that will be contained in the *DSM*-V, due to be published in 2012 to 2013. Some scientists want to eliminate the diagnosis of schizophrenia altogether, contending that it is not a distinct diagnostic entity.

ORGANIZATIONS TO CONTACT

The editors have compiled the following list of organizations concerned with the issues debated in this book. The descriptions are derived from materials provided by the organizations. All have publications or information available for interested readers. The list was compiled on the date of publication of the present volume; the information provided here may change. Be aware that many organizations take several weeks or longer to respond to inquiries, so allow as much time as possible.

American Psychiatric Association (APA)
1000 Wilson Blvd.
Ste. 1825
Arlington, VA 22209-3901
(888) 357-7924
www.psych.org

The APA is an organization of professionals working in the field of psychiatry. The association works to advance the profession and to promote the highest quality care for individuals with mental illnesses and their families. Additionally, the APA educates the public about mental health, psychiatry, and successful treatment options. The organization publishes the twice-monthly newsletter *Psychiatric News*, as well as several journals, including the *American Journal of Psychiatry* and *Psychiatric* Services.

Dana Foundation: Dana Alliance for Brain Initiatives (DABI)
745 Fifth Ave., Ste. 900
New York, NY 10151
(212) 223-4040
fax: (212) 593-7623
www.dana.org

The Dana Foundation is a private philanthropic organization with principal interests in brain science, immunology, and arts education. The Dana Alliance for Brain Initiatives (DABI) is a nonprofit organization of neuroscientists committed to advancing public awareness about the progress and promise of brain research and to disseminating information on the brain in an understandable and accessible fashion. DABI organizes and coordinates the international Brain Awareness Week campaign and presents *Gray Matters* radio series on Public Radio International. Dana Foundation publications include *Cerebrum*, an online journal of opinion with articles and book reviews exploring the impact of brain research on daily life and society, and *Brain Work*, providing the latest in neuroscience research six times a year.

Mental Health America
2000 N. Beauregard St.
6th Fl.
Alexandria, VA 22311
(703) 684-7722
fax: (703) 684-5968
www.mentalhealth america.net.

Mental Health America (formerly known as the National Mental Health Association) is a nonprofit organization dedicated to helping all people live mentally healthier lives. The organization educates the public about ways to preserve and strengthen its mental health; fights for access to effective mental health care; fights to end discrimination against people with mental and addictive disorders; and fosters innovative mental health research, treatment, and support services. Mental Health America issues several e-mail newsletters such as *The Bell* and produces several fact sheets and informational documents.

National Alliance on Mental Illness (NAMI)
2107 Wilson Blvd.
Ste. 300
Arlington, VA 22201-3042
(703) 524-7600
fax: (703) 524-9094
www.nami.org

The NAMI is a national grassroots mental health organization that seeks to eradicate mental illness and improve the lives of persons living with serious mental illness and their families. The NAMI works through advocacy, research, education, and support. The organization publishes a periodic magazine called the *Advocate.*

National Alliance on Research for Schizophrenia and Depression (NARSAD)
60 Cutter Mill Rd.
Ste. 404
Great Neck, NY 11021
(800) 829-8289
www.narsad.org

Originally incorporated as the American Schizophrenia Foundation, NARSAD is dedicated to mental health research. The alliance supports innovative research that tries to unravel the complexities of schizophrenia, depression, and other psychiatric diseases. The organization's publications include *Breakthroughs*, which provides stories about NARSAD-sponsored researchers, and the *NARSAD Research Quarterly*, which provides a forum for researchers to present the results of their studies.

National Institute of Mental Health (NIMH)
Science Writing, Press, and Dissemination Branch
6001 Executive Blvd.
Rm. 8184, MSC 9663
Bethesda, MD 20892-9663
(866) 615-6464
fax: (301) 443-4279
www.nimh.nih.gov

The NIMH is the leading agency of the U.S. government concerned with mental health issues. The mission of the institute is to reduce the burden of mental illness and behavioral disorders through research on mind, brain, and behavior. The NIMH publishes various booklets, fact sheets, and easy-to-read materials on mental health issues.

Schizophrenia International Research Society
545 Mainstream Dr.
Ste. 110
Nashville, TN 37228
www.schizophrenia
researchsociety.org

The mission of the Schizophrenia International Research Society is to bring together researchers in schizophrenia and related disorders in order to exchange ideas, facilitate research, and promote education about schizophrenia. The *Schizophrenia Bulletin* is the official journal of the society.

Society for Neuroscience (SFN)
1121 Fourteenth St. NW
Ste. 1010
Washington, DC 20005
(202) 962-4000
fax: (202) 962-4941
www.sfn.org

The SFN works to provide professional development activities and educational resources for neuroscientists and to educate the public about the findings, applications, and potential of neuroscience research. The organization has several online publications, including *Brain Backgrounders*, an online series of articles that answer basic neuroscience questions, and *Brain Briefings*, a monthly two-page newsletter explaining how basic neuroscience discoveries lead to clinical applications.

Substance Abuse & Mental Health Services Administration (SAMHSA)
Center for Mental Health Services
1 Choke Cherry Rd.
Rockville, MD 20857
(240) 276-1310
fax: (240) 276-1320
www.samhsa.gov

SAMHSA, part of the U.S. Department of Health and Human Services), seeks to ensure that people who suffer from mental health or substance abuse disorders have the opportunity to live fulfilling and meaningful lives. The agency's vision is expressed as "A Life in the Community for Everyone." SAMHSA works to expand and enhance prevention and early intervention programs and improve the quality, availability, and range of mental health and substance abuse treatment and support services in local communities across the United States. The agency publishes the bimonthly newsletter *SAMHSA News* as well as various recurring statistical reports on mental health and substance abuse.

Treatment Advocacy Center
200 N. Glebe Rd.
Ste. 730
Arlington, VA 22203
(703) 294-6001/6002
fax: (703) 294-6010
www.treatmentadvo
cacycenter.org

The Treatment Advocacy Center is a national nonprofit organization dedicated to eliminating barriers to the timely and effective treatment of severe mental illnesses. The center promotes laws, policies, and practices for the delivery of psychiatric care and supports the development of innovative treatments for and research into the causes of severe and persistent psychiatric illnesses, such as schizophrenia and bipolar disorder. The Blog on the organization's Web site provides articles written by Treatment Advocacy Center members and research results from the organization's studies.

FOR FURTHER READING

Books

Xavier Amador, *I Am Not Sick I Don't Need Help*. Peconic, NY: Vida, 2000.

Julio Arboleda-Flórez and Norman Sartorius, eds., *Understanding the Stigma of Mental Illness: Theory and Interventions*. Hoboken, NJ: Wiley, 2008.

Melody Carlson, *Finding Alice*. Colorado Springs, CO: Water Brook, 2003.

Michael Dunn et al., *Our Voices: First-Person Accounts of Schizophrenia*. Bloomington, IN: iUniverse; 2008.

Michael Foster Green, *Schizophrenia Revealed: From Neurons to Social Interactions*. New York: W.W. Norton, 2003

Kim Hopper, Glynn Harrison, Aleksandar Janca, and Norman Sartorius, eds., *Recovery from Schizophrenia: An International Perspective; A Report from the WHO Collaborative Project, the International Study of Schizophrenia*. Oxford, UK: Oxford University Press, 2007.

Brooke Katz, *I Think I Scared Her: Growing Up with Psychosis*. Bloomington, IN: Xlibris, 2004.

Elyn R. Saks, *The Center Cannot Hold: My Journey Through Madness*. New York: Hyperion, 2007.

Jeffrey Schaler, ed., *Szasz Under Fire: The Psychiatric Abolitionist Faces His Critics*. Chicago: Open Court, 2005.

Kurt Snyder, Raquel Gur, and Linda Wasmer Andrews, *Me, Myself, and Them: A Firsthand Account of One Young Person's Experience with Schizophrenia*. Oxford, UK: Oxford University Press, 2007.

Patrick Tracey, *Stalking Irish Madness: Searching for the Roots of My Family's Schizophrenia*. New York: Bantam, 2008.

Els Van Dongen, *Worlds of Psychotic People: Wanderers, Bricoleurs and Strategists*. New York: Routledge, 2004.

Periodicals and Internet Sources

Eduardo Aguilar, Samuel Siris, and Carmen Leal, "Can Atypical Antipsychotics Reduce Suicide Risk in Patients with Schizophrenia?" *Psychiatric Times*, April 2008.

Robert Drake and Susan Essock, "The Science-to-Service Gap in Real-World Schizophrenia Treatment: The 95% Problem," *Schizophrenia Bulletin*, June 2009.

Seena Fazel et al., "Schizophrenia and Violence: Systematic Review and Meta-Analysis," *PLoS Medicine*, August 11, 2009.

S. Ghose et al., "Differential Expression of Metabotropic Glutamate Receptors 2 and 3 in Schizophrenia: A Mechanism for Antipsychotic Drug Action?" *American Journal of Psychiatry*, June 2009.

Steven P. Hamilton, "Schizophrenia Candidate Genes: Are We Really Coming Up Blank?" *American Journal of Psychiatry*, April 2008.

Virginia Holman, "Not Like My Mother," *Prevention*, March 2008.

S. Horváth and K. Mirnics, "Breaking the Gene Barrier in Schizophrenia," *Nature Medicine*, May 2009.

P. Lichtenstein et al., "Common Genetic Determinants of Schizophrenia and Bipolar Disorder in Swedish Families: A Population-Based Study," *Lancet*, January 2009.

Medical News Today, "Kalirin's Role in Learning and Memory," November 22, 2007. www.medicalnewstoday.com/articles/89562.php.

Tina Hesman Saey, "You Are Who You Are by Default," *Science News*, July 18, 2009.

Bob Salsberg, "Boston Cops: Psych Patient Stabs Doc, Is Shot Dead," Associated Press, October 27, 2009. www.ap.org.

Schizophrenia.com, "Interview with Michael Mack," July 3, 2006. www.schizophrenia.com/sznews/archives/003594.html.

Carol Smith and Daniel Lathrop, "State Pays in Blood for Flawed Mental Health System," *Seattle Post-Intelligencer*, September 4, 2008. www.seattlepi.com/local/377671_mental04.html.

Renato Souza, Silvia Yasuda, and Susanna Cristofani, "Treating Schizophrenia with DOTS in Developing Countries: One Size Does Not Fit All," *PLoS Medicine*, September 2007.

Jacob Sullum, "Thomas Szasz Takes on His Critics: Is Mental Illness an Insane Idea?" *Reason*, May 2005. www.reason.com/news/show/32186.html.

Toronto Globe & Mail, "Patients' Rights Frustrate Families," March 12, 2009.

INDEX